Ginny's Christmas Wish

LYNN STORY

I0525190

November Fifteenth

Ginny

It was a perfect day for a funeral, the sky was overcast and the clouds and fog creating a somber mood as if the earth itself was morning the loss of Ophelia Graham. The procession of mourners dressed in black, carrying umbrellas and huddled deep into their coats against the cold were silhouetted against the gray sky as they made their way to the burial site for the graveside service. I was dressed like all the other mourners, black heels, which considering how soft the ground was, turned out to be a mistake, a black dress, black wool coat and a scarf. The wind would not allow for a hat today leaving my hair to become tangled and out of control. The wind was also stinging my face and making it impossible to hold back the tears.

My mother, Ophelia Graham, had fought a courageous battle against cancer for three years, every time she beat it, it came back worse than the time before, this last year she had declined quickly, and I moved home from New York to care for her rather than have her live in some impersonal care facility. In the end it was too much to handle and I had to hire a hospice nurse to come in daily to help with her medication and care. There had been few visitors in her final days, but today it looked like half of Gates Point had turned out to honor her. My mother was fairly well known in the community she was a beloved member of the garden club and the literacy council. As I stood waiting for all to assemble and the pastor to begin, I shivered. The kind of cold you get from standing outside with wet feet and temperatures hovering around forty-two degrees. But the cold wind and drizzle wasn't the only reason I was shivering; I was dreading the afternoon to come when people would stop by the house to pay their respects and provide an endless parade of casserole dishes. But, what could I do? I couldn't refuse them and insult my mother's friends. Besides mom loved a party and would be so happy to see so many people stopping by the house. She had made me promise not to have some boring memorial service with too many flowers and even more speeches. No, she wanted one last party. She wanted all her friends together and to remember all the good times. I hoped today was what she wanted because I was having a hard time celebrating anything. I was alone now, I felt abandoned and scared. Not to mention it would probably take a year to get through all the food that people had already dropped off earlier in the day, much less what was sure to come.

I made it back to the house with enough time to change out of the black dress and heels and into a pair of black slacks with a black polka dot blouse and a comfortable pair of flats before the guests arrived. Some of the women from the garden club volunteered to help with the food and keep the guests properly fed. I found myself in the living room talking to some of my mother's friends when the guests began to arrive in earnest, and it became my defacto reception point. I greeted the guests before ushering them off to Ms. Brown where they would be offered refreshment and pushed through the dining room and into the den and back out to the foyer after they had stayed the acceptable amount of time. The faces began to blur after an hour, they were all very kind, but I was having a hard time remembering all the names and faces. I doubted very much, any of them would remember my name after today, so I didn't feel so bad.

"We will miss your mother; she was a treasure."

"I don't know what we will do without your mother."

"I'm so sorry for your loss, dear."

"Hi, I'm Arlo," A young man with a mop of unruly dark hair stood in front of me with his hand outstretched. He was dressed in a suit and tie, but I could tell he wasn't used to wearing a suit on a regular basis. He looked vaguely familiar.

"Ginny Graham," I blinked as if bringing him into focus and shook his hand.

"Yes, I know," he smiled, "I live across the street, I used to do odd jobs for your mom, remember?" He stooped down a little to make sure I was looking at him.

"Oh, yes of course. I'm so sorry."

"Don't be," He looked around at all the people, "I'm sure it is a bit overwhelming today."

I stared at him for a minute grateful that someone understood even if he was a stranger. I did vaguely remember him stopping by to say that he had cut the grass or trimmed the hedges. Mom had always been the one who chatted with him and slipped him a few folded bills. I never knew how much mother was paying him and I worried that he might be trying to scam an elderly lady. Mom assured me that he was a fine young man just trying to make ends meet and that she had known his parents Mr. and Mrs. Michaels before they moved away, I forget to where, I remember her telling me I needed to look for the good in people and be more trusting. But my mother was had lived here after my father retired from the Army and she knew just about everyone in town. I was focused on too many things at the time to press mom further. I just knew that the yard work was just one thing I didn't have to worry about at the time.

"Oh yes, of course." I plastered a smile on my face. "It is so nice of you to stop by."

"Your mother was always very good to me," He looked at the que forming behind him. "Well, again I'm sorry for your loss." He quickly moved on.

I had an urge to talk him for a few more minutes there was something sincere in his eyes. But there was someone new shaking my hand and kissing my cheek and telling me how wonderful my mother was, which of course I already knew. The procession of people felt like it would never end, and I was getting tired. I hadn't eaten anything all day and I was starting to feel lightheaded.

Finally, the people began to leave, and the garden club started to wrap up the food and put it away. And just like that, I was alone in my mother's big Victorian house. Faced with being completely alone I stood in the middle of the living room looking around wondering what to do next. Every day of my life for the past year was consumed with my mother, I no longer had a purpose in my life. I didn't have to make dinner for her and I. I didn't have to go to the kitchen and pull out all the medication she needed to have at bedtime. Instead I walked to the kitchen and took all the meds out of the cabinet and sorted them out based on how they needed to be disposed of appropriately. Then I found some macaroni and cheese in the fridge and put that in the microwave for dinner. I was too tired to do anything else. I finally drug myself upstairs and stopped at mom's bedroom door half expecting to see her there. The silence now deafening as I touched the bed but couldn't bring myself to sit on it as if the cancer was contagious and a living thing. As tired as I was, I began ripping the linens off the bed racing down to the laundry room I shoved them in the washer and turned on the hot water adding bleach to the detergent. I went back upstairs going over in my mind the next several days having to go through all mom's clothes, shoes, jewelry, deciding what to keep and what to give away. But I couldn't do it tonight. I walked across the hall to my room and changed into a t-shirt and shorts. Sitting in the middle of my bed and cried like a little girl who was lost and alone in the world. My mother and I had been close. We didn't have spats like some mothers and daughters; we were best friends. Because, we moved ever few years I didn't have close friends, but I always had my mom. We had a tradition whenever we moved to a new place, we would find the local movie theater and the best place to get a milkshake. And our first Saturday we would go to a matinee and lunch and explore our new home.

I missed my mother and my friend, and I hope that if there was an afterlife that my mother and father were together and happy once again.

November Sixteenth

Ginny

Out of habit I got up early the next morning to check on my mother. I was used to getting up to prepare her breakfast before the nurse came by to bath her and help her dress. I was going to have to develop a new morning routine. Maybe I could start practicing yoga again. It had been something I did regularly when I lived in New York, but this past year the days were filled with so many other things I had gotten out of the habit. But for today I would have to settle for preparing myself a proper breakfast and dress for work at Bumboat Books. I prepared a hot breakfast and coffee and sat down at the kitchen table eat. It was a different experience to not have to grab a cereal bar on the way out the door in a rush always on the cusp of being late for my part-time job. I sat thinking about my future and did I want to return to New York? I could probably get my old job back at the publishing company, but I had gotten used to the slower pace here and I really hadn't missed the hustle and bustle of city life. My job at the bookstore wasn't going to be enough to maintain the house and allow me to eat and I needed a new plan. Being an only child there was no question of what would happen to my mother's property. Mother had shown me the will and there were some donations to be made to her favorite charities but that would still leave me with a sizable nest egg, which I had no intention of using unless things became desperate. But for the moment I had a job even if it was part-time and I needed to get to there this morning and worry about the rest later.

"Good Morning Ginny, are you sure you should be here today?" Wendy, the owner of Bumboat Books asked looking up as I came through the door.

"Yes, I can't sit at home in that big empty house."

Wendy gave me a sympathetic look although I knew she was glad I came in; we had a lot of work to do for the holidays. "So, I'm going to get the Thanksgiving sale flyer mailed this afternoon." I reassured her as I took off my coat and headed to the back of the store where there was a long worktable normally used for sorting books although today it was being used for folding and addressing flyers.

"Do you need any help?"

"No, I think I've got it." I wanted to immerse myself in something to keep my mind off all the things I had to do at home, like going through mother's closet or the attic.

Wendy felt the need to keep the conversation going, "Are you going to decorate the house for the holidays?"

"I hadn't really thought about it. I mean it was always beautiful when mom decorated it, but it seems sort of pointless this year with just me there." Honestly, I wasn't sure I could bring myself to decorate, it would just be another reminder that I was alone in the world. I had always enjoyed the holidays and felt so sorry for those individuals who get depressed during such a magical time of year. Now, I totally understood and like those people I used to pity, I just wanted to stay in my house and hide from the world until the holidays were over. The reminders of happier times were just too painful. They were just a date on the calendar, a deadline for sales flyers and social media ads. Christmas was looming just off in the shadows like the ghost of Christmas past and I was Marly avoiding everyone and everything that reminded me of my mother.

Wendy looked at me with pity. "Don't be ridiculous, you love the holidays, and it was just your mom there for years and she still decorated it. Besides that, house is a staple on the historic home tour for the garden club."

"The garden club, are you trying to turn me into a spinster already?" I rolled my eyes at the mere mention of those sweet but fussy friends of mom's.

Wendy laughed, "No, but it would be a shame to see it bare and dark, I'll come help you if you want. We could invite Becca and the others to come help too." Wendy suggested inviting other employees from the store.

"I don't know I have to think about it." I could tell Wendy wanted to say more but she didn't.

What if Wendy and Becca came over? Maybe it would keep me from sitting around feeling sorry for myself. Or would it just remind me of the traditions that were now gone with my mother?

Sitting at home alone wouldn't change the fact that I would never again spend a Christmas drinking wine and decorating the tree with my mother. Or that we would binge as many Christmas movies as possible on Christmas day, a tradition we started after my father passed. Drinking peppermint hot chocolate and opening presents.

"I'm not committing to anything just yet, but I'll think about it." I said as Wendy was about to turn and go back up front.

"That's the spirit!"

Having successfully delt with Wendy I turned my attention back to the computer and the flyers laying on the table. I needed to concentrate on folding these flyers and getting them in the mail for the holiday sale.

Arlo

Arlo Michaels was up hours before dawn to dress and walk to the diner to meet his boss Captain Shorty Johnson for breakfast before heading out on the fishing boat for the day. The front that brought the clouds and rain the day before was supposed to be moving out, it would take the rain with it, but it was going to leave cold temperatures. Arlo dressed warmly and packed his duffel with warm dry clothes, he was preparing to spend a couple of nights out on the boat harvesting bay scallops. Gates Point is famous for its seafood; products from the bay were sold around the world and it was men like Arlo that went out everyday rain or shine, no matter the temperature to bring in the fish, oysters, crabs and scallops. Just about the only thing that could keep men like Arlo and Shorty off the water was a hurricane. You didn't make any money if your boat was tied up at the dock. The hours were long, the work was hard, but Arlo never minded hard work, the money was good, and he loved watching the sunrise over the water.

"Morning Arlo," Shorty called out from the counter at the center of the diner.

Arlo walked over and took a seat next to him, "Morning Captain,"

"Looks like the weather will hold today,"

Arlo nodded as the waitress put a cup of coffee in front of him. "Looks like,"

"You are having the usual, Arlo?" The waitress asked impatiently.

"Yes, ma'am."

The waitress nodded and moved on. The diner catered to the fishermen; they were open before five in the morning and closed after lunch. Their busiest time of the day was the breakfast crowd. By the time the fisherman were fed and pulling out of the harbor, the office workers and the rest of the working world was just getting up and ready for their coffee for their morning commute.

"You ready to be out for the long haul?" Shorty asked Arlo, even though he already knew the answer. Arlo was his best worker.

Arlo nodded to his duffel. They had a short window to go out and get as many scallops as they could. It was going be twenty-hour days and to make the most of it, they would stay on the boat taking shifts sleeping and working. It was grueling work, but the payoff was worth it, and Shorty would give them a few days off as a bonus when they returned.

The waitress brought his breakfast and Arlo enjoyed the eggs, bacon and pancakes, knowing it would be the last hot food he'd have for several days. He would live on sardines, crackers and coffee on the boat. He brought along a bag of oranges to share with others.

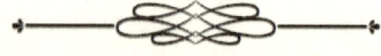

Ginny

It was after closing when Wendy came into the work room, "why don't you go home, we can work on these tomorrow."

"I'm almost done, but you go ahead I have my key I will lock up when I leave."

Wendy sighed. Any other time Wendy would have insisted, she was a good boss and didn't work her employees too hard or take them for granted. But I think she knew I needed to work right now was not in a rush to run home to an empty house.

"Ginny what are you doing for Thanksgiving?"

I had been focused on Christmas and the sale flyers I hadn't really given much thought to Thanksgiving, "When is it?"

"It's next week, I know you've had a lot on your plate lately, why don't you come to my house and have dinner with us, Becca and her boyfriend will be there." Wendy offered.

"Oh, I don't want to impose."

"There is always room for one more at our table."

I appreciated the invitation, "Can I think about it?"

"Of course, you can." It's an open invitation you are always welcome."

"Thanks," I was relieved when I finally heard the door click closed behind Wendy. I wasn't sure what was worse the looks of pity or the constant need to make sure I was taken care for all of the holidays. It didn't matter how much I told Wendy I would be okay, she didn't believe me and insisted that I be distracted in some way. I was truly grateful for her concern but, it was just too early to be making plans. I still had so much to do. I needed to go through mom's things and putting it off wasn't going to make it any easier.

When I was finally done with the flyers I walked up and down the aisles of books. I loved books, the way they felt, the way they smelled and the possibilities they held to transport you to another place and time. If I had the attention span right now to read a book I could do with a little escapism. Anything that could transport me away now to a place where there no pain of loss, a place where you didn't feel alone even if you were alone. I decided to walk over to the self-help section and looked at books on grieving, I selected one and flipped through the first few pages, replaced it and selected another and glanced through the first two chapters. I repeated the process with every book on death and grieving I could find, and what I discovered is that they were all pretty much telling me the same thing. Grieving was an individual process it was different for everyone and even with help I would have to find my own way through. In other words, nothing I didn't already know. Wendy had been right, it was time to go home, I cleaned up the work area, and locked the door behind me on my way out. I was fortunate that Bumboat Books was within walking distance of my mother's house. It had been a wonderful advantage when I first moved here. I didn't own a car and even though my mother's car was available, I was used to walking or taking the bus wherever I needed to go. Tonight, on the way home, I decided to walk past the house down to the seawall near the marina. I had been drawn to the water since moving here and enjoyed the salt air, the cries of the gulls and watching as storms rolled up the Chesapeake Bay. I wasn't ready to go home and sit in an empty house, so despite the chill in the air, I decided to sit along the seawall listening to the water slap up against the riprap and the stare off into the night and the lights of the distant shore until they blended with the stars. I'm not sure how long I sat there but when by my legs were numb from the cold, I decided I had sat there long enough. I managed to get up and limp home. I was too tired, and my mind was too distracted, to focus on getting anything done around the house, so I took a cup of chamomile tea and a decorating magazine upstairs to my room. Maybe, I was tired enough to fall asleep.

November Nineteenth

Arlo

We stayed on the boat for three days straight, the weather was cold the wind making it worse, but we got a good haul of scallops. So much so that Shorty agreed to give us a few days off before Thanksgiving. I planned to sleep through most of them. I was chilled to the bone and certain I would never be warm again. The clouds that had been haunting us out on the bay finally came to shore and flurries started to fall as I walked back to my apartment. It didn't matter though, I was already too cold to feel them, I stumbled into my apartment and began stripping off my clothes and soon as the door was closed on my way to a hot shower. I hoped that I might thaw out enough to get some sleep.

Ginny

The flyers having been completed and Wendy dropping them in the mail today, I had the day off and decided it was time to get started going through mother's things. The house was clean and tidy with everything was in its place as was mom's way, but I still felt compelled to investigate every nook and cranny in the house. I opened the door to check the mail and was shocked to see a man standing on the porch about to knock.

"Oh, hello,"

It was the good-looking handyman I and met at the funeral. He looked like I had startled him as much as he had startled me. "I, um thought I would stop by and see if you needed anything," he shuffled his feet looking a little nervous.

It was cold outside and there was a light dusting of snow on the ground.

"It's freezing out here, won't you come in."

He and stepped inside and I closed the door tight behind him and shivered.

"Would you like something warm to drink? I've got tea, coffee, cocoa."

"I don't want to impose, I just thought I'd drop by and see if you needed help with anything. Ms. Graham, uh you mother, used to hire me to put up the decorations outside and since we seem to be getting an early winter, I thought I would see if you want to get a head start."

"Oh, that was very nice of you, but I hadn't really given much thought to decorations. I'm not even sure where they are." I hadn't gotten around to looking for them yet.

"Oh, well they are up in the attic, I can get them for you if you like."

I bit my lip, I wasn't sure that I wanted to drag it all down, then I would feel obligated to put them up and I hadn't given it any more thought. But I had a feeling that I wasn't going to get out of it.

"Arlo, isn't it?" I asked motioning for him to take a seat in the living room.

"Yes, that's right, Arlo."

"Well, to be honest, I wasn't really considering decorating this year. I mean it is just me and with mom gone there doesn't seem to be much point."

He nodded and looked disappointed. "Of course, you have to do what you think is best. I just know there are quite a few things that are normally hung outside and I thought if you had decided to use them you would want some help."

"Can I ask you something?" He nodded to me, but he looked like he wanted me to do anything but ask him a question.

"Did you know my mother well?"

"Yes, since she moved here."

I thought about it a minute. My parents moved here when I was in college. I never lived here with them although I came home for summer breaks and visited them many times over the years and I didn't remember ever meeting this young man before and we had to be close to the same age. "Really, did we ever meet back them?"

"I don't think so," He looked perplexed. "But I didn't start doing odd jobs for here until a couple years ago. My parents moved to Florida about the time I graduated college. I didn't want to move with them and that is when I started renting a room across the street and started doing odd jobs in the neighborhood for extra money."

"And what do you do when you are not doing odd jobs?"

"I work on a fishing boat."

"Even this time of year?"

"Oh yeah. The only thing that will stop us from going out is a nor' easter or a hurricane."

I wasn't sure what else to say, when I started speaking again it was like I couldn't control the words coming out of my mouth. "Well, okay I guess you could bring them down and I'll go through them. I'm not sure how much I want to put up just yet."

"Okay, sure, I'll just go upstairs if that is okay."

I don't know what made me say it. I felt my cheeks reddening, "Um, yeah sure."

I watched for a moment as Arlo starting walking slowly towards the stairs. Then I got up and followed up.

"Do you need any help bringing down the decorations?" I asked stupidly.

"Well, only if you want to, I could hand them down to you."

"Sounds like a plan."

"I put them all in one spot to the left so it will be easy to get them, but I will warn you there are quite a few boxes and things."

I tried to remember last Christmas, but mom had been so ill, and I really hadn't been paying attention to the decorations, Arlo must have come then to put them up, but everything was such a blur I honestly didn't remember.

"Have you spent many Christmases in Gates Point?" Arlo called down through the opening in the ceiling.

"No not really, I was here last year of course, but I honestly don't remember much about it other than mom being too sick to get out of bed."

Arlo's head appeared in the opening, "first box coming down." I climbed halfway up the stairs and took it from him.

"Yes, I imagine everything from this past year is probably a blur for you, I am sorry that your last memories of your mother in this house are painful ones."

I stared up into his warm brown eyes, a stray curl falling down over his left eye.

"Well, luckily there are many more happy memories than sad ones." I said taking the box and setting it on the floor.

He smiled down, "that's good to know, hang on to that." He disappeared again and returned a moment later with another box.

"Hopefully, this year you will get to enjoy more the festivities we have. Gates Point is transformed at Christmas."

I smiled at his childlike excitement. "Really, how so?"

"Oh, it's amazing! There is the lighted boat parade along the waterfront, there is the big Christmas parade downtown. There are Christmas trees everywhere, the historic district actually put fake façade on the buildings and transforms it into a Dickens village with street performers that perform a Christmas Carol right on the sidewalk and pull in passing shoppers. It's a lot of fun." He laughed.

Before I knew I found myself being swept up in his enthusiasm. It was hard not to be.

An hour later than had all the boxes down and the hallway looked like it was moving day with all the boxes neatly stacked. Each one was neatly labeled and had an inventory list taped to the top. It wasn't her mother's handwriting. "Did you do all of this?"

"Oh yeah," he shrugged, "I would spend hours going through all the boxes looking for specific ornaments or something for you mom, so I decided to make an inventory sheet to save myself some time."

I had to laugh, "I don't blame you, she used to do that to me too. Hey, you want something to drink, I could use a break."

"I have iced tea, coffee, soda, and water,"

"Tea would be fine."

I grabbed the pitcher out and set it on the counter while retrieving two glasses from the cabinet. I poured us each a glass. We sipped their tea and an awkward silence filled the air.

Finally, I broke the silence, "How long have you lived here?"

"All my life."

"Really?" Having moved so much as a child I was fascinated and a little envious.

"Yeah,"

"Have you ever traveled?"

"Sure, on vacations and stuff I've traveled to a few places, but I've never lived anywhere else. Not like you."

"Like me?"

"Yeah, you mom told me your dad was in the Army and you guys moved every few years. It sounds exciting but rough at the same time."

I wondered what else I mother had told him.

"Well, you're right. I mean, I didn't appreciate it as much at the time. But I am lucky I got to live in some of the different places that we lived and experience different cultures and viewpoints. On the other hand, I never really had any close friendships."

"Did you ever miss having a best friend growing up?"

"Oh yeah. I'd move to a new school most of the kids there already knew each other for years, they viewed outsiders like me suspiciously and it took a while for them to warm up to you, but by then we had orders and were moving again. It was a cycle and I guess I got used to it." I thought of Brenda, a friend I had in the fourth grade. "The easiest schools were the ones overseas because all the American kids were in the same boat, and we all immediately gravitated to each other."

"Wow, some of my friends I've known since elementary school. And the ones I'm not friends with today, there are still a bunch of guys I know from school and run into them at the store or a just around town."

"More tea?" I offered, "I can't imagine knowing that many people in one place.

"I suppose it probably seems kinda backwater to you, living in one place my whole life."

"Not at all, what is it like?"

"Well, it offers a sense of belonging I suppose. A place that feels like home and is. But it has its disadvantages too,"

"Really? Sounds good so far."

"Well, it is great that you have lifelong friends and when you go out you always run into someone you know. Someone who is familiar, but on the other hand everyone knows everyone else's business. So that can be a little annoying." He laughed.

"Sounds comforting, though. You know there is always someone around that can lead a hand if you need it."

He shrugged, "I guess. I mean the grass is always greener, right?"

"Well, you could travel and see the world now if you wanted to, couldn't you?" I realized I actually didn't know anything about Arlo beyond what he did for my mother. He could have a wife and children for all I knew or worse he could be some sort of felon, didn't he say he lived in an apartment in the old converted house across the street, maybe it was a halfway house for people trying to reenter society.

"Yeah, I could travel around, I have a passport and everything, but I don't know," He shrugged, "it doesn't sound like much fun to go by yourself."

"Hmm, that is true I suppose, I mean it is nice to share your experiences with someone who enjoys the same thing I decided maybe I should know more about Arlo before I had him do anything else with the decorations.

"Tell me more about working on the boat." I tried to sound casual.

"You know the ones you see going out in the mornings."

"Yeah, what sorts of things to you fish for?"

"We bring in crabs, mostly, but certain times of the year we bring in bay scallops, that is where I have been for the past three days. We went out and brought in bay scallops and the captain gave us a couple of days off."

"Sounds like really hard work."

"It is, I'm not planning on doing it for long. I enjoy being on the water and the money like I said is good, so I am saving as much as I can for right now, so that I can maybe start my own business one day."

I had to admit I was impressed. "A fishing business?"

"No probably not. I get tired of coming home smelling like something even the cat wouldn't drag in."

I laughed. It felt good to laugh again. "Do you have family here?"

"No, my parents retired to Florida, my brother moved to Texas, so it's just me, that is why I can rent that little efficiency from Ms. Potter across the street. It isn't much but it is cheap and I'm not there most of the time anyway. I'll get a nicer place someday." He looked wistful for a brief moment.

"What about you? Are you going to stay here in Gates Point for a while at least?"

"Yes, I thought I would. I really can't imagine going back to New York now, but I probably need to find another job."

"Why, don't you like working at the bookstore?"

"I do and Wendy has been more than understanding about my schedule so that I could take care of mom and her appointments, but if I am going to keep this house, I need a little more income to keep up with the maintenance and the taxes."

Arlo nodded. "I can understand that, what do you want to do?"

"Well, in New York I worked in marketing for a publishing company, but there aren't too many publishing companies down here, so I guess I need to find a marketing job in another field."

"Why not start your own company?"

I laughed half-heartedly, "I wouldn't know where to begin."

"Well, the city has some really good resources for small businesses, I bet you could go talk to someone and get something set up. You could work from home." He waived his arms in a sweeping motion. "They have grants and things to help you get started."

Arlo was certainly full of surprises and I was feeling better about the fact that he was probably not a dangerous felon. "How do you know so much about all of this?"

"Well, I don't want to be hauling in scallops and crabs the rest of my life." He smiled.

"No, I suppose not." I chided myself for underestimating him. "Thanks, I'll think about that."

We sat and talked for hours before Arlo announced he should probably go.

"Oh, I didn't realize what time it was. Thank you so much for the help." I wasn't sure if I was supposed to pay him for bringing down the decorations or not and it felt a little awkward. "Can I give you something for getting the stuff down out of the attic?"

Arlo held up his hand in protest, "No, not at all. I am glad to help. Let me know though when you're ready to have me put the wreaths and lights outside."

"Okay, sure. Uh maybe this weekend?" Again, my mouth was speaking without checking in with my brain first. It was like it had a mind of its own when it came to Arlo and I tried to clamp my mouth shut.

"This weekend would be great."

I smiled. "Okay,"

Arlo headed for the front door. I stood holding it open wishing he didn't have to go. If I was honest, I had enjoyed talking to someone about something other than illness or death.

"I'll see you this weekend," Arlo stepped out onto the porch.

"Okay," I watched him walk down the steps and retreat across the street to his apartment. There were worse things in life than having Arlo come over and help with decorating the house. I honestly didn't care about the decorations one way or another, but it was a legitimate excuse to have him around.

November Twenty-First

Ginny

Saturday morning Arlo was back, and I was happier than I should have been to see him. I was up early and had showered and dressed not knowing what time Arlo might appear. I wanted to be ready. I had this weird feeling in the pit of my stomach, and I didn't like it. I was supposed to be in mourning not fawning over my mother's handyman. We carried the boxes out onto the porch and Arlo retrieved the enormous wreaths that would be hung on the eaves of the house. I worked on the smaller wreaths on the windows and the garland along the rails of the porch.

"Hello, there!" A voice called from the bottom of the front steps.

I looked up to see a woman who appeared to be in her mid-fifties and dressed in a conservative suit with pearls and heels. "Hello,"

"I'm Anita Miller, I was a friend of your mother's."

For some reason I felt an instant dislike for this woman. Maybe it was the forced smile; the fake sincerity. The fact that she claimed to be a friend of my mothers, but I was sure I had never seen the woman before. She paused as if waiting for me to invite her up on to the porch, when it became apparent, I wasn't going to invite in her up, she forced a smile. "I'm a real estate agent, I just wanted to stop by and give you my card. Now that your poor mother, may she rest in peace, has passed on, I'm sure you'll be wanting to sell this big house." She smiled again a little too sweetly, "If you need any help with that please let me know."

I looked down at the card I kept my expression as neutral as possible, "Thank you, if I decide to sell, you'll be the first person I think of, thanks for stopping by." I forced my own smile.

Arlo came down from the ladder and, I could tell by his expression he wasn't a fan of the well-dressed real estate agent. Anita Miller turned without another word and walked back to her car, her heels clicking on the sidewalk as she went.

Arlo picked up another large wreath as he watched the car pull away, "What was that all about?"

I was practically fuming. "Oh, she just wanted to stop by and give me her card." I thrust it at him. He took the card and looked down at it then handed it back without a word.

"Do you know that woman?"

"I only know who she is."

"I don't think I like her."

Arlo smiled, "Not many people do."

"She seems pushy."

"She is," He nodded in agreement smiling to himself. "I'll bet she has had her eye on this house for years."

"Well, she can just think again." I marched into the house and tossed the card in the trashcan.

"So, you're staying?" Arlo asked when I returned to the porch.

"I'm certainly not going to let the likes of her within an inch of this house." I crossed my arms defiantly. At that moment I decided I was staying in Gates Point, no one was going to force me out and I certainly wasn't going to hand over my mother's dream home to a greedy real estate agent.

It was nearly five o'clock before we finished with the outside of the house.

"Are you hungry?" I suddenly had the urge for a deep-dish pepperoni pizza.

"Yeah, sure."

"Wanna go to Sal's for pizza and beer?"

Arlo's face lit up. "You bet!"

"Perfect, I need carbs and cheese." I laughed looking for my purse. "It's a long walk in the cold, should we drive?"

"Driving might be best. And if we drink too much beer, we'll just get a ride share home." I suggested.

"I can't imagine getting impaired on the watered-down beer they serve at Sal's but okay."

"I just might order a beer in a bottle." I argued. The draft beer wasn't bad at Sal's it was just the brands they had on tap were weak in my opinion, but then I had been introduced to beer when we lived in Germany, so I preferred the stronger beers.

Arlo laughed. "Okay then. You do that and I'll drive you home."

"It's a deal."

November Twenty-Second

Ginny

The next day, while I was working in the back of the bookstore, I heard the unmistakable voice of Anita Miller enter the store. Wendy was with another customer so I started towards the front to see if I could offer assistance.

"Hi Anita, I'll be with you in a minute." Wendy called out.

"No need, I'm just here to pick up my magazine."

Relieved that Wendy had greeted her I stayed out of sight and imagined Anita making her way to the magazine rack. I wondered if she was looking for a copy of Snob and Garden, I could see from the back that Anita had found what she was looking for and was headed to the counter to pay, but Wendy was done with her other customer and went to the counter to assist Anita.

"How are you today?" Wendy said as she tapped on the keypad of the register.

"Wonderful, how are you? How is business?"

I rolled my eyes; I was sure Anita Miller could care less about Wendy's revenues for the month, she probably had her eye on the store, it was in a perfect location on the edge of the waterfront area and the business district.

"Oh, just fine, always a big rush before the holidays."

Anita looked around at the near empty store surprised. "Really?"

"Oh yes, busiest time of year." Wendy said cheerfully.

"Well, this is a wonderful location, I'm not surprised." Anita sniffed.

I balled my hands into fists, I wanted to run out there and punch Anita Miller in her stuck-up face. "Ginny Graham works here part time, doesn't she? Anita asked as she accepted the receipt from Wendy.

"Yes, she does. Why?"

"I was just wondering if you knew what her plans were. I'd love to market that house for her." Anita's voice dripped with false sincerity.

"You'd have to ask Ginny."

"Yes, well, thanks for the magazine." Anita said brightly.

I heard the little brass bell on the door ring indicating Anita had left so I stepped out of the back. "She really gets under my skin." I was seething.

"Just ignore her, everyone knows she's a fake."

"Really?"

"Oh yeah," Wendy laughed. "She puts on airs, but she was the biggest tart when we were in school and everyone knows it. One of her ex-husbands set her up in the real estate business because she couldn't keep a regular job. And now she tries to pass herself off as someone who only handles high-end property."

"She came by my house last night and gave me her card."

"Are you serious?"

"Yes,"

"She's got balls I'll give her that." Wendy shook her head.

"How many ex-husbands does she have?"

"Oh, I think she is up to four now, but honestly I've lost count."

"Wow and I haven't had a date in nearly two years, and she has had four husbands." I had to laugh.

"Well, now I'm depressed, thank you very much." Wendy laughed and headed back to the books she was shelving.

"You're welcome."

"Ginny, have you thought about what you are going to do?" Wendy said over her shoulder.

"I'm planning on staying, but don't worry Wendy I promise if anything changes, I'll let you know."

"Well, I'm glad to hear it, my sales are the best they have been and I'm sure you should get all the credit. You have done so much for our marketing,"

"Actually, I was wondering if I should try and start my own marketing business."

"That would be amazing you should do that, and I will be your first client."

"Are you serious?"

"Absolutely."

"Okay, well I'll give it some thought." Maybe Arlo was right, I decided to go down and talk to someone in the Gates Point

Economic Development office when I got off work.

Arlo

I was enjoying my last day before going back out on the water. I had enjoyed helping Ginny with the decorations. Going out for pizza and beer afterwards was something I hadn't expected but was glad that things had worked out the way they did. I started thinking more about the conversation we had about starting her own business. Maybe I needed to start thinking about that for myself. I've been saving money for a few years now and I knew I didn't want to work on a boat for my entire life, not that it wasn't a good job, it was an honest living, but I had always dreamed of bigger plans. But over time those plans had changed and now I wasn't sure what I wanted to do. One thing I was sure of though, was that whatever I did I wanted it to include Ginny. It surprised me how strong my feelings where for her in such a short amount of time, but when something is meant to be it is just meant to be. She was an open and honest person, she didn't mince words, but she was careful not to hurt the other person she cared about how people felt, and I like that about her. Today too many people were so wrapped up in their own lives they didn't think about what they said or did and how it might affect someone else. Or maybe some did think about but still didn't care. I wasn't sure which was worse. One thing I was clear on I didn't want to work the boats anymore, but the bigger question was, what did I want to do. I had a business degree. Maybe I should work on a masters and get an MBA, but then what? I couldn't imagine working in some corporate office or worse sitting in a cubicle. I needed to start exploring my options. I needed to discover what I enjoyed doing and then find a way to make a career out of that. Yeah, that was going to be easy.

As I left my apartment and walked around to the front of the house to the street, Ms. Potter was sitting out on her porch in her ever-present house dress and robe with a cigarette burning between her fingers.

"I hope you aren't going to start having a lot of girls visiting." She called out to me.

"Excuse me?" I wasn't sure what she was talking about.

"That girl," she pointed across the street to Ginny's house.

"Okay, not sure I follow."

"Well, if you're going to start having a lot of girls come over, I hope you keep it down."

"Don't worry, I'll be quiet." I shook my head and walked out to the sidewalk. I always knew she was a busy body, so I wasn't sure why I was surprised at her words other than I had never had Ginny or any other girl in my apartment the entire time I rented from Ms. Potter. I couldn't afford to find another place to live just now so I would just have to try and ignore her for the time being.

I walked down to the diner for coffee. I sat mulling over my options. I didn't mind hard work, but I needed a change from this current job. I wondered if I could expand the handyman business like building decks and things. That didn't really give me a warm feeling either. I stared out the window, what was I going to do with the rest of my life.

My phone buzzed I was surprised to see a text message from Ginny.

"I had fun last night; I'm going to the city today to talk to someone about starting my own business."

"I had fun too, let me know how it goes.

"Stop by later and we'll talk about?"

"It's a deal, I'll bring dinner."

"See you then."

I paid for the coffee. I felt like a little of the weight from my shoulders had been lifted by the text from Ginny. Things didn't seem quite so daunting as they had only moments ago. I was anxious for the afternoon to pass so I could see her again. I found myself walking along the water my mind filled with thoughts about what to do with the rest of his life and what to take to Ginny's for dinner. I would have to pick something up, I only had a hot plate and a microwave in my apartment so I couldn't prepare anything for her there.

Ginny

I left the store at noon in a hurry, munching on a granola bar on the way to my car to drive to the city offices in downtown Gates Point. I had never had a reason to drive to this part of town in the year that I had lived here, and it was quite intimidating. The traffic was much more congested in this part of town, the buildings were taller I soon realized that parking was a challenge as well. It was as if when I drove across the Apollo bridge, so named for the space missions, that I was in another city all together. It wasn't quite on the scale of New York, but it was close enough for me to be glad I lived in the older section of the city. I found a parking spot a block away from City Hall. I took a deep breath as I got off the elevator on the sixth floor.

"Hello, can I help you?" A pleasant young man greeted me as I entered the office.

"Yes, I am thinking of starting my own business in Gates Point, but I'm new here so I was wondering if there was anything you could tell me about what I need to do to get started."

"Absolutely, let me get one of our business specialists to meet with you, may I have your name?"

"Ginny Graham."

"Thank you, here is our small business packet, you can glance through that while you wait."

He handed me a blue folder.

"Thank you, I took it and sat down to wait." I flipped through the pages of what was essentially a magazine. There was a CD in the left pocket of the folder as well. It all looked promising.

"Ms. Graham?"

"Yes,"

"I'm Darlene Montgomery, small business specialist, won't you come in?"

I followed the well-dressed young woman down the hall and into an office with a beautiful view.

"So, you want to start up a business in Gates Point, tell me more about that."

I sat down in a guest chair and felt a little uncomfortable without having an actual business plan in my hand and began to wonder if this visit was pre-mature.

"Well, I moved here a year ago and I've been thinking lately about starting my own marketing business. I am just doing a little research at the moment; I don't have a business plan to share with you at the moment."

"That's okay, we can get to that later."

"We have a couple of different programs depending on the type of business and the location. Have you thought about a location yet?"

"Well, I have a huge house and I live alone so I have space enough there."

"A home occupation, okay. How many employees do you think you will need to start off with?"

"I was thinking one other person besides myself for a start."

The young lady nodded. "We have some excellent business properties, that are available at very reasonable rates for new businesses, plus we have a grant program to help you get your technology set up started."

I perked up at the mention of a technology grant. "Really?"

"Yes, we have a program to convert home occupations into some of our aging commercial space to help breathe new life into some areas around the city, part of that is a very reasonable rate for the first two years and a technology grant which you can use for equipment and advertising costs."

"That sounds wonderful, what else do I need to be thinking about, I assume a business license."

After an hour I left feeling more confident about the idea of starting my own business. I was armed with a ton of information and I couldn't wait until this evening to tell Arlo everything I had learned.

Evening of November Twenty-Second

Ginny

That evening the doorbell rang and I knew it was Arlo before I even got to the door. He was punctual if nothing else.

"Hi," I smiled opening the door.

"Hi, I brought Chinese take-out, I hope that is okay."

"That is perfect, and it smells wonderful." I stepped aside to let him in. He was carrying two large brown bags.

"Wanna sit here?" I pointed to the larger dining room table instead of the smaller kitchen dinette.

"Sure," he set the bags on the table and began opening them.

I ran to the kitchen to get plates; I hadn't realized how hungry I was until Arlo opened the bags and the wonderful smell of food came wafting out.

"I brought chop sticks just in case,"

"Even better, what would you like to drink?"

"Iced tea if you have it."

"Of course." I laughed. I had learned quickly after arriving that you didn't dare get caught without a pitcher of sweet tea in the refrigerator when guests stopped by. "Holy cow, how much food did you bring?" I said as he removed container after container from the bags.

"Well, I wasn't sure what you liked so I got a couple of different things."

"Okay then."

We sat down to eat, passing around General Tso's chicken, lo mien, and fried rice, spring rolls, and Moo Goo Gai Pan.

"How did the meeting go downtown today?"

"Oh, it went really well. First of all, I've never been downtown before, so that alone was an eye-opening experience."

Arlo laughed, "yeah it is a different world isn't it? I'm sorry I should have warned you."

"It's okay I managed; I just wasn't expecting it. But, the people in the development office were really helpful and gave me a packet of information. And a lot to think about."

"That's good, isn't it?"

"Oh yeah, they have a program for new businesses to move into empty commercial space rather than start up a home-based business, and it includes a technology grant."

"Really?"

"Yeah, and I'm thinking if I do this, I am going to have to hire at least one person. It is becoming clear the more I look into this I can't do it alone. So, I need to think about how much money I have available to invest in this venture."

Arlo sat listening as I prattled on, "I told Wendy that I was considering it she said she would be my first client." I paused to take another bite of food. Then I put the chopsticks down.

"Arlo?"

"Yes?"

"You're not eating or talking, is something wrong?"

"No, I was just thinking."

"Anything you want to share?"

"Well, yeah, but I'm afraid you'll think I'm crazy."

"Why would I think that?"

"Because it is kind of a crazy idea."

"Crazier than me moving here and starting a business when I really don't know anything about Gates Point, and the only people I know are you, Wendy and the people who work in the bookstore."

"Yeah, it is a little crazier than that."

"Okay, then let's hear it."

"Well, you know we were talking before and I said I didn't want to be a fisherman my whole life and lately I've been thinking more and more about making a change. I have my business degree and I have been thinking about putting that to good use or maybe getting my masters."

"I understand the working on the boats is hard, but I would think it would be hard to give up those sunrises on the water."

"Well, I'd rather be able to enjoy them while relaxing maybe on a nice little sailboat or something."

"Really?"

He put his chopsticks down for a moment, "Yeah, have you ever been sailing?"

"No, I haven't?"

"What? No way!"

"Yeah never got into it. I don't think I even had friends with boats."

"How is that possible? I mean of all the places you've lived around the world and you never went sailing anywhere?"

"No," I shrugged, "I guess the opportunity just never presented itself."

"Well, we will have to see what we can do to change that." Arlo grinned at me.

"I guess growing up here you have a lot of experience with boats and things."

"Oh yeah, my brother and I started learning to sail when we were very young, we both competed some. My brother stuck with it longer than I did. He got into some sailing regattas with real prize money." He shrugged.

"And you got into commercial fishing." I finished for him.

"Yeah, something like that. My father tried to get me to move to Florida when my parents retired, but I just can't do it."

"I bet Florida is beautiful and I'm sure they have plenty of boats down there."

"Yeah, but it isn't the same."

I let it go for now and started a new line of questioning. "How often do you see your parents?"

"I go down to visit them about once a year, my dad tries to talk me into moving down there every time I visit, so I quit visiting them as often."

"I've never been to Florida, but is sounds nice, mild winters and lots of beaches."

"Yeah, I guess." He played with a noodle on his plate.

"So, I think we got side-tracked you were telling me about an idea you had."

Arlo looked at me and I got the feeling he had hoped to avoid the topic.

I tried to reassure him so he wouldn't think I was prying, "you don't have to tell me, that is okay."

"I just don't want you to think I am crazy or that I had some sort of ulterior motive."

"Why would I think that?"

"Well, while you were talking earlier about your experience downtown, I thought maybe you could hire me, and we could start your business up together." He looked uncomfortable like he wanted the floor to open up and swallow him.

I sat back and thought about it for a minute.

"I shouldn't have said anything." Arlo stood up and I was afraid he was going to leave.

"Hey, don't go. I think that is a great idea, but I was thinking we could be partners."

He turned and looked at me in surprise. "What?"

"Yeah, partners." I smiled at him.

He sat back down and stared at me.

"How would that work?"

"Well, we can talk about what strengths each of us bring to the table, we can decide what kind of clients we want and what areas we want to focus in. I think you would be a great asset; you know the city better than I do and certainly more people." I realized I was talking fast I, but I was excited at the prospect of actually starting my own business. And I liked spending time with Arlo.

Arlo sat staring at me, his face a mask, I couldn't tell what he was thinking. Maybe I had taken it a step too far. "I'm sorry I get carried away sometimes."

"No, that is okay. I think it is great. I just didn't really expect you to actually want to bring me on."

"Why not? I already know you're a hard worker. You care about people because you helped my mom out and you didn't have to," I paused because I almost said 'and I like spending time with you' but I caught myself.

"So, what do we do next?" He asked.

"Clean up this mess." I laughed.

"Okay."

We cleaned up all the food containers and dishes. We were putting away the last plate when Arlo turned to me,

"Are you serious about us starting this company together?"

I looked at him, his warm eyes, the unruly mop of hair and wondered if this was a mistake. Would I be able to keep things professional? He was too good looking for his own good, but he seemed to be completely oblivious to the effect he had on me. Maybe because he wouldn't have any problem keeping things professional.

"Yes, I am."

He blew out a breath and seemed to relax a bit, "Okay, when you're ready to discuss the business plan, I have some savings I can contribute to the start up."

I had to admit I was excited and scared all at the same time. "Okay, and I have the money from mom's insurance. I might have to keep working at the bookstore until we get on our feet."

"Well, let's look at the numbers before we commit you to working two jobs." He smiled a perfectly charming smile.

"Agreed."

"Well, I should probably be going. See you tomorrow?"

I smiled up at him, "Yes, tomorrow."

Arlo hesitated for a half a heartbeat, but then turned and left.

November Twenty-Third

Ginny

I could barely sleep my thoughts were filled with ideas for the new business. I spent the night tossing and turning before I finally gave up. Turning on the bedside lamp, I looked around. I couldn't just sit in bed, so I started pacing around the room, but that wasn't enough, so I put on a robe and slippers and headed downstairs. I decided tea was the only cure for this bout of insomnia. I sat at the kitchen table waiting; it seemed like the water was taking an infinitely long time to boil. Finally, the kettle started emitting steam and I took it off the stove before it's little whistle blew. With tea in hand I padded out onto the porch to drink it. The air was cold, but the sky was clear, and the stars were beautiful. I wasn't a very religious person and I wondered now if there was any truth to loved ones looking down from heaven. What would my mother think about all of this? I was reasonably sure she would be happy I was keeping the house. I wondered if I was crazy for starting up a new business, and was it even crazier to start it with a business partner I had only just met at mother's funeral? Well, I've done crazier things in my life, like spending a summer on the beaches of Mexico and packing up everything and moving to New York after graduation determined to make it in marketing. I had been so broke when I first got to New York, if I had had a car, I would have lived in it. But instead I lived in a tiny apartment with two other people from the marketing firm where I had finally landed a job. It hadn't been the glamour I imagined it would be. The marketing company was housed in an old office building with smoke stained walls and bars on the windows even four floors up. We had worked on the worst ad copy I had ever seen. It was a year before I moved to a slightly bigger firm and inched my way to success. I was nearly at the top of my game and my career was on schedule when mother had gotten sick. I tried to provide as much care for her long distance and had made several trips home. I finally had to quit my job, give up my coveted rent-controlled apartment and moved to Gates Point.

With my thoughts returning to the here and now, I realized it how cold it was out here, and I shivered involuntarily. I hated the thought of going in, and leaving the stars and the peacefulness of the night, but my mother's voice echoed in my head, 'you'll catch your death out here, Virginia, come in the house' so I went inside, put the cup in the sink and climbed the stairs to the second floor. Maybe the tea would kick in and I would be able to sleep now. At least obsessing over the new business kept me from thinking about the holidays too much and was a welcome distraction to how much I missed my mother.

Arlo

I was restless and suddenly my small efficiency felt too small. I have never been claustrophobic. I was used to working in tight spaces on the boat, but tonight the walls were closing in on me. I stepped outside for some fresh air and to feel the expanse of the night sky. I felt the urge to step around the side of the house and stare across the street, it looked as if there was a light on downstairs, but the light was dim which meant it was in the back of the house near the kitchen. Just then the front door opened, I instinctively took a step back not wanting to be caught, as if my emotions were visible in the dark. I could just make out a silhouette as Ginny came out and sat on the porch. I stood there fighting the urge to walk over and sit with her, clearly, she was restless as well, but I didn't want her to think I was stalking her or watching her house at all hours of the day and night. I felt like I was invading her privacy and I should go back inside but no matter how hard I tried to will my legs to carry me back into the apartment they wouldn't listen. So, I stood in the shadows watching her I regretted not putting on a coat before coming out here because it wasn't until she went back inside was I able to return to the warmth of the apartment. I hoped she wasn't up at this hour because she was having second thoughts about us being business partners. It had seemed like the perfect idea at the time. Why else would she be sitting outside alone on her front porch? I couldn't imagine going a day without seeing or talking to her. She had become important to me so quickly it was frightening. I was used to my freedom, coming and going as I pleased, and I had no ties here and no one to keep me accountable for anything other than my own common sense. I had always enjoyed this lifestyle which hadn't included much beyond working on the boats or odd jobs and sleeping suddenly it didn't seem like enough.

"Shit!" I laid back on the bed and stared into the darkness, who was I kidding I had nothing. Not a close friend, not a place of my own not even a car. I had always been nervous and shy around girls, so I never learned the art of flirting or dating like some guys. Ginny didn't have any use for a guy like me beyond a business partner. And I was lucky if she even considered me that.

It was three o'clock and the alarm went off. I dressed and rode my bike to the diner for coffee and to meet up with Shorty before heading out for the day.

Ginny

I woke up at eight o'clock Sunday morning feeling refreshed. I had slept later than usual but then I had been up half the night roaming the house like some restless spirit. I didn't have to work at the bookstore today, so I could relax and enjoy a cup of coffee and work out my priorities for the day. I still needed to sort through mother's clothes, and I wanted to work on the business plan for the marketing business but some of that would have to wait until I talked with Arlo a little more. I wasn't really sure what I should include in the business plan and I hoped he would be able to help with that.

So, it was time to stop procrastinating and get to work on going through mother's things. I took a deep breath and went downstairs in search of boxes or bags to put her clothes in. By noon I had filled three bags with clothes, another with shoes and handbags and lugged them all downstairs to the car to drive them to the donation center. On my way home I stopped at the local grocery store and spied Anita Brown in the produce section, I tried to avoid her, but it was too late, Anita had spotted me. I gritted my teeth as Anita sauntered over wearing a fake smile plastered on her face.

"Ginny, so good to see you,"

"Ms. Miller," was all I could manage to say and keep a civil tongue in my head. I had no reason to be rude, but this woman just brought it out in me for some reason.

"How are you holding up dear?" Anita said in a low tone putting a hand on my arm. It took everything I had not to pull away from her and I'm sure from a distance anyone would have thought we were good friends.

"I'm as well as can be expected, I suppose. I've just dropped off some things at the donation center."

Anita made a sympathetic noise, "You poor dear," she shook her head then looked around conspiratorially.

I looked around as well and noticed another woman approaching the produce section and eyeing Anita suspiciously.

Anita continued on in a motherly voice, "I couldn't help but notice you had a handy man helping you around the house, do you think that is a good idea for a young single woman such as yourself?"

I blinked at her, at first, I wasn't sure what Anita meant or who she was referring to, then I remembered Arlo had been there when she had stopped by the drop off her business card.

"Do you mean Arlo Michaels?"

Anita looked disapprovingly. "Yes, that is who I mean."

"Arlo and I are friends, I'm not sure what you are implying." I felt my temper was starting to flare up, just then the other woman approached us and focused on Anita.

"Anita! How are you?" The woman said in a way that put Anita's fake sincerity to shame. I bit my lip to keep from laughing.

Anita looked a little flustered, "Kay, how are you?"

Clearly Anita wasn't happy to see this woman.

"I'm doing well, I haven't seen you in so long or any of your signs over in the Garden District I was hoping you hadn't gone out of business."

Anita's face turned bright red and I had to look away to keep from laughing out loud. Clearly this other woman had Anita's number. I didn't know everything about Gates Point, but I knew the Garden District was a very historic and prestigious neighborhood. The kind of place I could only dream of living.

"Yes, well I've been keeping busy." Anita stammered.

The woman named Kay looked over at me. "Hello, I'm Kay Dandridge," She held out a hand. I accepted and smiled taking an instant like to Kay Dandridge, "Ginny Graham."

"Ginny is Ophelia's daughter; I've been trying to convince Ginny here to let me handle the sale of that beautiful old Victorian."

Kay looked over at me with interest, "Oh, what a shame to sell such a wonderful home."

"I'm not, actually. I've decided not to return to New York, but to stay here and start my own business." I heard myself say.

"That is wonderful, what business are you in?"

"Marketing."

Anita blanched and I took more pleasure in it that I should have.

"Did you work in marketing in New York?" Kay asked.

"Yes, I did for several years, I only came home to take care of mom in her final year."

"I'm sorry for your loss. Look here is my card, when you're up and running give me a call."

I looked down at the card and was surprised to see that Kay Dandridge was the owner and CEO of the largest employer in the city, Port City Industries. I also made a mental note to add business cards to my list of things I was going to need. "Thank you, I'll do that." I smiled.

"Anita," Kay nodded and moved away.

Anita mumbled something about having to be somewhere and moved away quickly.

I loved how Kay Dandridge and bested Anita at her own game. I finished the shopping and found that I couldn't' wait to tell Arlo about the experience. Feeling a renewed excitement, I went home and spent the rest of the afternoon researching and drafting up a business plan.

November Twenty-Fourth

Ginny

I had been at work for an hour when Wendy came in through the backdoor of Bumboat Books.

"Morning, you're here early."

"Morning Wendy. Oh, I had a new idea for a flyer and wanted to get started on it."

"Have you thought anymore about Thanksgiving?"

I had forgotten all about it. "Uh, not really. I guess I should start getting ready for that, huh?"

"It's in three days if you don't have a turkey already you are going to pay and arm and a leg for one." Wendy eyed me as she hung up her coat. "Which is all the more reason you should come to my house for dinner; you can just bring wine or something."

"Yeah, um if I were to come to dinner would it be okay if I brought a plus one?" I felt stupid for bringing it up. I should have just declined the invitation altogether. There it was again; my mouth was operating independently from my brain at the moment.

Wendy's eyes lit up, "A plus one? Really? Who, tell me everything!" She pulled up a metal folding chair and sat down next to me.

"It's not what you think, we are just friends." I thought for a moment and said quietly to myself 'and business partners.'

"Hmm, spill." Wendy was on the edge of her seat.

"His name is Arlo. I met him at mom's funeral. Well officially, I'm sure I must have met him before, but I don't remember."

"Why would you have met him before?" Wendy looked confused.

"He was mom's handyman."

Wendy leaned in, "A handyman? This is good."

"Wendy you are getting it all wrong."

"Okay then tell me and don't leave anything out."

"There is nothing to leave out," I began fiddling with a pen on the table. "We are just friends, he came over and helped me hang up Christmas decorations, which by the way you insisted that I should do."

"Yeah, okay so then what happened?"

"Well, he has come over for dinner a couple of times."

"Yeah, go on." Wendy was practically salivating.

"And nothing that is it. He lives alone across the street and we enjoy each other's company."

"Is he a good kisser?"

"Is this high school? Really?"

Wendy would not be put off. "Yes, really."

"Well, I have no idea," I sniffed, "We haven't kissed."

Wendy looked completely disappointed. "What? Why not?"

"Because, like I said we are just friends."

"I thought young people today were uninhibited by old fashioned rules and stuff, I thought you guys went around hugging and kissing each other all the time."

I laughed out loud, "Where did you hear that?"

"It was on some TV show the other night, one of those reality things were a bunch of young people live together and everyone was doing it with everyone else."

I laughed so hard tears formed, "That so-called reality show is to fake!"

"Well, yes bring your 'friend'" Wendy smiled and patted my shoulder. I don't think she believed anything I told her about Arlo. But she would see for herself on Thanksgiving.

Promptly at six o'clock the doorbell rang, and I knew it had to be Arlo I practically ran to the door.

"Hey," I sounded breathless even to myself.

Arlo grinned. "Hi, did I come at a bad time?"

"No," I grabbed his hand without thinking and practically dragged him into the house.

"What's going on?" Arlo laughed stumbling along behind me.

"So, I went to the grocery store today,"

"Did you get the turkey for dinner?" Arlo asked sensibly.

"No, but I'll get to that part in a minute,"

"Okay," He laughed.

"The point is I ran into Anita Miller in the produce section and she started her usual fake speech about how I was doing, blah,

blah, blah."

Arlo frowned, "You didn't punch her, did you?"

I sat back, "No, why would you think I would punch her?"

"Well, I know you don't like her."

"So, you think I go around punching people I don't like?"

"I wouldn't blame you if you did, she is annoying."

"Okay, can I just tell my story, please?"

"Yes, I'm sorry go ahead." I could tell he was trying not to grin.

"So, she was going on and on, telling me it was basically unseemly for me to have a handyman over," I paused for effect, "meaning you, because I was a single young woman in the big ol' house alone."

Arlo eyes widened, "She said what?"

"I know right? So anyway, this other lady came over and I guess she knows Anita and how she is,"

Arlo interrupted again, "Everyone does."

"So, this woman gives Anita a taste of her own medicine and asks her why she isn't listing any houses in the Garden District and said she thought Anita had gone out of business or something."

"Oh, I bet that set Anita off!" Arlo laughed,

"Yeah you should have seen her face! And the other woman turned to me and introduced herself and I told her I was not selling my house and that I was planning on staying here and starting up a marketing business, and she said when we were ready to give her a call!" My excitement was at the tipping point.

"So, who was this hero?"

"Look!" I handed him Kay's business card.

Arlo took the card and blinked, then looked at me. I was bouncing in my seat, and then back down at the card. "Are you freaking serious?"

I nodded biting my lower lip.

"This is amazing!"

"I thought so too, so I came home and was all excited and I started drafting up the business plan and researching some of what we would need for startup funds. I hope you don't mind that I did this before you got here."

Arlo smiled, "I don't mind, let's go over what you have so far together."

We sat for hours poring over what I had drawn up, Arlo making suggestions here and there. Finally, we took a break and I made sandwiches for dinner, and we worked until midnight.

"Oh my gosh, look at the time, and you have to be up early to go to work, I'm so sorry." I hadn't realized how late it was, I wasn't tired at all.

"I'm okay,"

"You'd better get some sleep."

"I'm not sure that will help actually, I'll just feel more tired with only a couple hours of sleep than if I didn't go to bed at all."

"Okay, want to watch a movie and eat ice cream?"

He looked at me puzzled for a moment. "Sure,"

"But, first, you were going to tell me something earlier about not getting a turkey for Thanksgiving."

I had forgotten all about that, "Oh yeah, well uh. Wendy invited us to her house for dinner and I was wondering if you would like to go with me." I suddenly felt awkward.

"Yeah, sounds like fun."

"Okay," I breathed a sigh of relief. I handed him the remote, "find us something to watch, but nothing scary. I'll get the ice cream."

"Okay." He turned on the TV and began flipping through the channels.

I took two bowls and sat down next to him on the sofa with my feet tucked under me.

"What are we watching?"

"Witches and vampires." He grinned.

"I thought I said nothing scary."

"Witches and vampires aren't scary, zombies, now those are scary."

I had to laugh, "Okay, okay, but if I can't sleep, you're going to have to sit up with me."

He studied my face and I wondered what he was thinking.

"Deal."

The movie turned out to be more of a romance between monsters than the unfettered killing of innocent people and when it was over, Arlo stood up.

"Well, I should probably get to work."

"Again, I'm sorry for keeping you so late."

"It's okay, I can take a nap when I get off work today, call you later?"

"Sure," I grinned.

I closed the door behind him, I probably needed to get some sleep too, but I was still too excited about the possibility of already having clients before the business was up and running.

Thanksgiving Day

Ginny

I was both excited and dreading the day with friends. I was missing my mom and the memories of Thanksgivings past flooded my thoughts. I hoped I would be able to get through the day without being too melancholy. I dressed and went downstairs to start cooking the oyster stuffing, with the oysters Arlo brought me. I also wanted to bake a chocolate pecan pie to take as well. Arlo had agreed to pick up the wine. We were going to meet here, and I would drive to Wendy's around noon. I turned on the radio, but it was filled with Christmas music already, I snapped it off impatiently. A quick look out the kitchen window, there was a thick frost covering the ground. I found the weather depressing for some reason. I sighed and poured a cup of coffee. I just wanted to get through the day and come back home and curl up on the sofa with a good book.

I lost track of time and was startled when the doorbell rang. I checked the clock; eleven thirty, it had to be Arlo. He was nothing if not punctual. He came in and glanced around and then followed me to the kitchen where I was packing up the stuffing and pie.

"You haven't started decorating yet."

I wanted to tell him that I had only decorated the outside to appease everyone who kept asking about it. I was under no obligation to decorate the inside where I was the only one that would have to stare at the constant reminders of how solitary Christmas this year would be and possibly every year from now on. But it wasn't his fault and I shouldn't take it out on him.

I forced a smile and answered his question, "no, not yet."

Arlo stepped close and put his hand on my arm, "Hey if today is going to be too hard for you, we don't have to do this I'm sure your friend will understand."

I was touched by the fact that he could see I was struggling. I gave him a small smile. "I'll manage. I have to start sometime."

"Yes, but it doesn't have to be today."

I had an urge to hug him at that moment. I really needed someone to reassure me that I was going to get through all of this, and everything would be okay. But of course, no one can tell you that. I smiled, "Thank you, that means more than you know."

He didn't smile back he studied my face as if he was looking beyond the forced smile, and into the pain I was keeping bottled up inside.

"Well, I guess we better go." I finally said.

Arlo broke away and picked up the dishes off the table. I grabbed the wine bag and headed for the door.

Arlo

I watched Ginny as we drove to Thanksgiving dinner, my heart was hurting for her. She clearly didn't want to do this, but I knew she wouldn't allow herself to sit at home and feel sorry for herself either. She was a strong woman, but even strong women need a shoulder once in a while. I didn't want to push her, but I hoped that she would let me help her. Standing in her kitchen earlier and seeing the pain in her eyes that she so carefully tried to hide. I just wanted to take her in my arms and protect her from it all. I wanted to take away her pain, I could only hope she somehow knew that. I wanted her to know that I would be there for her if she needed me. I was afraid to say the words out loud. I didn't want to risk the rejection; we had a budding friendship and a business partnership forming I didn't want to risk losing all of it. We pulled up in front of Wendy's house. I looked over at her and smiled.

"I'm here for you," I said softly.

She smiled back, "I know. Thank you."

It was the best I could do at the moment and I knew it was all she could do. We both took a deep breath and walked up to the front door.

Ginny

"I'll get it." I heard Wendy's voice through the door as Arlo and I stood in the freezing cold. I was used to the cold in New York but somehow Gates Point felt colder.

Wendy opened the door smiling, she reached out and hugged me and then pulled me into the house. "I am so glad you came! Hello, you must be Arlo." Wendy smiled at him and gave him a quick hug. I had to giggle at the look of surprise on Arlo's face.

"I'm Wendy, I run the bookstore." Wendy was dressed in jeans and a sweater with a picture of a turkey, "Please come in, here, I'll take all of that to the kitchen."

Wendy gave Arlo one last appreciative look before leaving us standing in the middle of the living room.

"Ginny!" Becca appeared and ran over to give me a hug.

"Hey Becca, I'd like you to meet a friend of mine, Arlo."

"Hi Arlo," Becca gave him a welcoming smile and shook his hand.

"Hello."

"Becca works at the bookstore and is going to school at night." I explained.

"Oh, what are you studying?"

"I'm an art major, mixed media art at the moment." Becca laughed "because there is absolutely no way to make a living doing that."

"Oh, I bet you could, just probably not in Gates Point." Arlo laughed along with her.

Becca leaned in conspiratorially "Yeah, I'm hoping to get an internship in New York, this summer, but don't tell Wendy."

Wendy reappeared just then, "Arlo do you like football?"

"Yes ma'am."

"Come on, I'll take you to the den, the boys are already in full football mode."

Arlo looked back at me. "It's okay, go ahead." I nodded.

He reluctantly followed Wendy.

I thought it was sweet of him to want to stay and make sure I was going to be okay.

When Wendy came back, she drug me into the kitchen.

"That is your handyman?" Wendy whispered.

"Yeah, why?"

Becca giggled.

"Do you think he will come over here and fix something for me?"

I looked at the two of them like they had lost their minds. "I'm sure he would."

Wendy laughed out loud.

"Girl, you need to open your eyes, he is gorgeous!"

"Oh, he isn't interested in me."

"Are you kidding?" Becca snorted.

"Yeah, we are just friends."

"Wish I had friends like that." Wendy said turning away from me and pouring a glass of wine.

She offered me a glass. I decided I needed it if I was going to get through this day.

Wendy and Becca started handing me plates to set the table.

"So, what does Arlo do when he isn't dragging boxes out of your attic?" Wendy asked.

"He works on the fishing boats down at the docks."

"Oh, that explains it,"

"Explains what?"

"All those muscles." Becca giggled.

I looked around afraid Arlo might overhear, "Shhhh!" I hissed.

"What?" Wendy tried look innocent.

"We are just friends."

"Why?"

"Wendy, seriously? Can you keep your voice down?" I fussed. "we are good friends and we are starting a business together."

"Really? Okay I had no idea. I apologize." Wendy was loud enough for Arlo to hear if he was listening.

The doorbell rang again.

"I'll get it," Becca called out.

More co-workers from the bookstore arrived the house was getting crowded and the hum of conversation was constant, but it was a distraction from the topic of Arlo and for that I was eternally grateful.

Finally, everyone arrived, and we settled at the table, Wendy stood, "I'm not a religious person so I will make a toast instead of fumbling my way through grace." She raised her wine glass, "Here's to new friends and family, and thank you for making this a wonderful Friendsgiving."

"To friends!" Everyone echoed.

We ate and shared stories and drank wine. After dinner Arlo drifted in once in a while for more beer for the guys in the den and would ask if I was okay. Each time I could feel Wendy's eyes on me, so I avoided her gaze.

Finally, the dishes and been washed and put away, everyone had their fill of food and drink and I was ready to go home. Arlo and I carried a plate of leftovers each at Wendy's insistence. She opened the door to find the weather had gotten even colder and snow was starting to fall.

"Wow, look at this, we almost never get snow at Thanksgiving." Arlo announced.

I looked up the heavy clouds blanketing the sky and for the first time today thought about the Thanksgiving festivities in New York it had snowed nearly every Thanksgiving while I stood along the parade route before jumping on a plane and flying home to see mom and dad.

"You okay?" Arlo asked once we were in the car with the heat blowing.

"I'm good, do you have to work tomorrow?"

"Yes,"

I was hoping he would say no and we could spend the day together. It was probably just as well. We pulled into the driveway and I offered him my plate of leftovers.

"You take it. You will need plenty of energy to keep warm on the boat tomorrow."

"I can't do that," Arlo shook his head and took a step back.

"Don't be ridiculous of course you can, and I insist." I stepped closer gently setting my plate on top of the one he was already holding and kissed him lightly on the cheek as snowflakes landed on his nose.

Arlo was too stunned to say much so he just smiled, "Okay then" and turned to head for home.

November Twenty-Seventh

Ginny

"Hi, Ginny."

"Morning Wendy."

"Hey, I drove past your house, I have to say it looks stunning with all those decorations up."

"Thanks! I had a good time at your dinner yesterday. Thank you again for inviting me."

"I hope Arlo had a good time." Wendy said with a wink.

"I think he did." I smiled but didn't give any more details. It was fun to keep her guessing.

She walked over and looked over my shoulder, "What are you working on?"

"Christmas flyers, this will probably be the last ones we mail out, we are running out of time. I'm going to schedule some social media ads and then the newsletter blast and then everything will be on autopilot."

"Then what are you going to do?"

"That will free up some time for me over the holidays to work on getting my marketing business up and running. I'm hoping to get it started for the new year."

"Are you going to leave me?"

"No, you said you wanted to be my first client, I just probably won't come in the store anymore to do the work."

Wendy looked disappointed, "Oh,"

"Hey, don't worry, we'll still talk every day and I'll come by to say hi and stuff. And I'll still do the flyers and the social media, just like I do now."

"Yeah, it just won't be the same without you here."

"You look like you have something on your mind." I said.

"I'm just worried you are turning into a workaholic."

"Wendy I was a workaholic before I moved here, I'm just getting back into my groove." I laughed.

Wendy changed the subject, "Are you going to the lighted boat parade?"

"The what?"

"The boat parade all the boat owners including some commercial boats decorate with Christmas lights and they sail down river, at the end there is a big Christmas party with the lighting of the tree ceremony down at the marina and tents with cider and food trucks."

"I think Arlo did mention something about that a while back, but I really hadn't given it much thought."

"You should come go with me, it is always so much fun, there will be carolers and everything; even fireworks."

"Wow, all that?" Thanksgiving was fun, but I'm not sure I was ready for more festivities. I had kinda hoped that doing the Thanksgiving dinner thing would have satisfied people that I was emotionally stable enough to get through the holidays without further babysitting.

Wendy sighed, "You're too young to be a scrooge."

"I'm not a scrooge at all, I think you should go and have a good time, I just have work to do if I am going to meet my January first deadline."

"But you're the one setting the deadline you can change it."

I smiled. "You are really sweet, don't worry about me, I have a big decorated house, I think that is all the Christmas cheer I can handle." I didn't bother with the details that the outside was just for show and the inside was completely unadorned.

Wendy sighed and went to work shelving new books. I knew she meant well, but I needed to grieve and recover in my own time. I didn't see how a boat parade was going to help with that or getting my business off the ground.

Later that evening Arlo came over bringing burgers from Smitty's.

"Hey, come on in let me show you what I've been working on." I said eyeing the white burger bags. "Oh, and I told Wendy today that after January first, I wouldn't be coming into the store anymore. But if she was still going to be our first client, I would continue to do her advertising for her."

"What did she say?"

"Well, she still wants us to do the advertising, but she was disappointed that I wouldn't be in the store every day." I shrugged, focusing on the laptop.

"I told Shorty, the same thing. That I couldn't work for him past the first of the year."

I looked up surprised. I guess I hadn't really expected Arlo to quit his job, but I was secretly happy that he did. "How'd he take it?"

"Well," Arlo carefully moved some folders to set the bag of burgers down and took a seat at the table. "I guess he took it as well as Wendy, he wasn't happy about it, but he said he understood."

"Wow, we are really doing this." I looked down at all the papers suddenly feeling a little scared.

"Yep, we really are." Arlo smiled. "Now look I'm starving can we eat first?"

"Sure, come on let's go into the kitchen." Ginny smiled and grabbed the bag. "What did you bring tonight?"

"I brought two super burgers, fries and apple turnovers. I hope you have something to drink because I forgot to order those."

"I have plenty of drinks. Should we have an adult beverage to celebrate?" I gave him a wicked smile.

"Absolutely, do you have beer?" Arlo unpacked the bag while I grabbed two beers.

I breathed deeply enjoying the aroma as Arlo unpacked the food. "God, I love the smell of those onions."

"I think the secret is they cut them and then put them in the fridge overnight. But they do smell good."

We toasted our future success with burgers and beer.

When we were done Arlo stood up, "Okay, show me what you have done so far today."

Arlo

"Hey are you ready?"

Arlo asked standing at my front door.

"Ready for what?"

"Oh, I thought you would be going to the boat parade, don't you remember me telling you about it?"

"Well, yeah, but I didn't really think about it."

Arlo looked disappointed, "Oh, okay."

"Are you going?"

"Well, yeah. Do you mind if I skip working on the business tonight?"

"No, of course not. Go have fun." I encouraged him; I didn't expect him to spend every waking moment at my dining room table.

"What about you, when are you going to have fun?"

"I am having fun, creating this business."

"Ginny this isn't New York you don't have to crush it every single moment of every day, you're allowed to have fun once in a while."

I frowned. "You don't think I know how to have fun?"

"No, I don't, truth be told, since I've met you all you have done is work at the bookstore, take care of your mom, and now you have thrown yourself into this project of creating the business."

I felt my temper rising up, mostly because I knew he was right. And he could see things about me that I clearly couldn't see. "I'm sorry if I like to stay busy and I don't meet everyone's idea of a grieving daughter!"

"I didn't say that."

"You didn't have to." I wanted to bite my tongue off but instead I just stared at him daring him to say something else.

"Okay, I'll see you later." He turned and walked down the steps out to the sidewalk.

I stood there stunned that he turned away so easily. I had wanted more of a fight. But, why? What was I hoping to gain by fighting with Arlo? I stood at the doorway watching him walk away. I noticed other people walking towards the marina I could join them; he wasn't so far away that I couldn't catch up and apologize. Instead I slammed the door. How could anyone expect a boat parade to replace my beloved Thanksgiving Day parade in New York, or that life with this life.

I stormed back into the dining room and stared at the papers spread across the table and screamed. I swept all the papers into the floor. Then staring at the mess, I had made of all my hard work I sat down and started to cry. I cried tears of anger for lashing out at Arlo, one of the very few friends I had in Gates Point and then tears of sorrow for the loss of my mother. I thought of how if she was here right now, she would know what to do, how I could fix this whole mess. But then if she was here there wouldn't be a mess.

I wasn't sure how long I sat there on the floor but, I didn't have any tears left. I picked myself up and went upstairs to the second-floor drawing room and looked out the large windows to see the lights of the boats. I raised the window and leaned out, I could hear music and the sound of crowds of people. I felt so foolish for how I had acted. I put on a coat and hat and walked down to the marina I doubted I'd be able to find Arlo in this crowd. The mood was festive, and people were greeting everyone cheerily and someone offered me a cup of cider from a stand. I smiled despite myself and accepted it. I walked around looking at all the different food vendors and crafts people. One tent was decorated with fake snow although it looked like we might have plenty of the real thing if these flurries continued; they were selling handmade Christmas stockings. I stopped and looked for a moment. There was one that was hand knitted and reminded me of a fisherman's sweater. I thought of Arlo. I bought it and planned to give it to him for Christmas. Carrying my purchase with me I felt the holiday spirit creeping into my soul despite my earlier bout of depression and selfishness There was a crowd forming near the dock and I could just make out a barge in the middle of the river. I walked up to the back of the crowd and asked a young couple what was happening.

"They launch the fireworks from the barge out there in the river, they are about to start."

"Thank you." I said and moved away skirting the edge of the crowd. As I inched towards the water, I saw Arlo standing off the side watching me.

I stopped in my tracks I felt embarrassed and my heart was pounding in my chest.

He gave me a small smile and walked over to me. "I'm glad you came."

"Listen Arlo, I'm so sorry. I don't know what came over me."

He shook his head, "There is no need to apologize, I'm the one who should apologize to you. I'm sorry for what I said."

"No, you are right, and I was acting like a spoiled brat."

He laughed. "I don't think anyone would ever accuse you of that."

Just then the first firework burst in the air above the river drawing our attention and the obligatory 'oohs and aahs' from the crowd.

Arlo put his arm around my shoulder and gave me a little squeeze and then released me smiling. But for that brief moment I felt safe, like everything would be alright.

Arlo and I walked home after the fireworks. Standing at the door I looked up at him, "Thank you for tonight. Again, I'm sorry for the way I acted. Let's take a break from the business until after Christmas."

"Are you sure?"

I nodded.

"Okay,"

"What are you doing for Christmas, are you going to Florida?"

"No, not this year."

"Oh, well you know if you don't have any plans, you're welcome to have Christmas dinner with me."

"Are you having the bookstore gang over?"

"No, it would just be us." I blushed realizing how the invitation must sound to him. But I couldn't take it back now.

"You aren't planning frozen dinners, are you?"

"No, I'm not really sure what I am planning, I guess it depends if you will be joining me or not."

"Tell you what, I'll come to dinner if you let me use your kitchen to cook it."

"You don't have to do that."

"I want to."

"Okay it's a deal."

Arlo bent down a little and touched my shoulder, "I'm glad you came out tonight."

"Me too."

"See ya," He said.

"See you." I whispered. I closed the door behind myself and looked at the mess I had made in the dining room. Not my finest moment.

December First

Ginny

Arlo hadn't been kidding when he told me that Gates Point embraced the Christmas spirit. I decided to go out and do a little shopping and there were indeed theater troupes roaming the sidewalks involving shoppers in their version of a Christmas Carol. I parked and walked around the historic district exploring the various shops. I found a wonderful art supply store and bought a few things for Becca. I was still at a loss as to what to get Wendy though. I decided to venture downtown. I was prepared for the traffic this time and I did want to see the large tree Arlo told me about. I crossed the bridge and found a place to park that was only two dollars an hour, which I thought was a bargain. I made it to the street level and headed for the shops and restaurants. I found the tree. It was quite a bit larger than the one down by the marina and there was an ice-skating rink in front of it. I felt like I was back in New York for just a brief moment. I stood watching the skaters for a little while. It brought back so many memories, the smell of popcorn from the street vendor made me smile. The trees lights were visible in the daylight and I enjoyed watching them change colors. There was a schedule posted for upcoming events at the tree. There was the obligatory Santa for the children to whisper Christmas wishes in his ear. It made me wish I had grown up here and envied what it must have been like for Arlo. There hadn't been any more snow since Thanksgiving, but today the clouds looked threatening, and I wished for a snowy white Christmas.

I turned my attention back to shopping and avoided the typical chain department stores and instead explored the specialty shops.

I found a very nice business card case for Arlo and had it engraved with his initials and a silk tie with boats on it. A reminder of his old life to carry with him into the new. I was on my way back to the parking garage after I had finally found a gift for Wendy when I saw a 'For Lease' sign in the windows of a beautiful tall office building. I stood staring up at the glass and steel wondering how many years it would take before I could afford space in a building downtown.

"Hello," A voice interrupted my thoughts. I blinked to see Kay Dandridge standing in front of me.

"Hello," I smiled.

"Its Ms. Graham isn't it?"

"Yes Ms. Dandridge, Virginia Graham." I held out my hand.

She shook it then glanced up at the building. "Are you thinking of leasing space in this building?"

"Oh no, I'm sure it will be a few years before we can afford a downtown address." I smiled.

"I see, well let's at least see what you get for your money downtown." She reached over and opened the door.

I stood there looking confused.

"It doesn't hurt to look, right?" She smiled.

I smiled back, "I suppose not." I followed her through the door. She walked past the security desk to the elevators and pressed the button for the second floor. I stood awkwardly wondering what I was doing in this elevator in a building I couldn't afford with one of the most powerful women in the city.

The elevator chimed and the doors opened. Kay stepped off the elevator and I followed her down the hall. The carpet was so thick it was like walking in soft sand. The hallway was decorated in warm colors designed to put you at ease. She stopped at a door marked 'Leasing Office'.

A young lady stood up when we entered, "Ms. Dandridge, so nice to see you."

"Hi Ellen, is Rich available?"

"I'm sure he is, let me check." Ellen sat down and pushed a button on the phone, "Ms. Dandridge here to see you." She hung up, "Go right in." She smiled.

I returned the young lady's smile and followed Kay. A large heavyset man opened the door to the right of Ellen's desk.

"Kay! How are you?" He held out his hand.

"I'm fine, Rich just fine. This is my new friend Virginia Graham; she is starting a new marketing firm here in our little city and I thought you could show her the space you have available for lease."

I smiled demurely and shook his big beefy hand. He had a better manicure than I did.

"Uh, well okay." He clearly didn't think I looked like I could afford the space either. I felt like a fraud standing here in my jeans and flats while Kay was dressed in a dark pinstriped suit.

"Let me just get the keys."

Within a matter of minutes, we were back on the elevator and headed to the twelfth floor. When we got off the elevator the hallway was even more luxurious. There was black marble with gold veins, but very tasteful not overwhelming. It all blended with the cream carpet and heavy wooden doors with gold lettering announcing names like Van Devender, LLC or Baker and Baker, P.C.

Rich turned to me, "The client has not vacated as yet, so their furniture is still here. They may be willing to part with some of it if you are in need."

"Thank you." Was all that I said not wanting to admit I was way over my head.

"How many in your firm?" He asked opening doors and blinds.

"We are just starting up, so two right now but I hope to have a third by the time we open our doors in January." It wasn't really a lie; it was a hope or maybe more like a dream."

"Well, this space will certainly give you a little room to grow, as you can see it has a state-of-the-art conference room," He picked up a remote and activated a drop-down screen.

I felt like a kid in a candy store.

"And what is the rate for this space?" Kay asked.

"Twenty-five dollars a square foot."

I nearly gasped out loud.

"Rich, why don't you leave the key with me and Ms. Graham and I will have a look around, is that alright?"

"Yes, of course. Just leave the key with Ellen." Rich smiled and was gone.

"Ms. Dandridge," I started as soon as the door was closed. "I hope I haven't given you the wrong impression,"

Kay held up her hand, "What that you are using your inheritance to start up this business? That you have a solid reputation in New York and paid your dues up there? That it takes a lot of courage to start your own business much less in a city that you are practically unfamiliar with?" She leaned against a desk that probably cost more than my beat-up car and folded her arms.

"How did you....?"

"Let's just say, my head of security knows how to do his research." She smiled. "After that day I met you in the market I offered you a chance to come talk to me, and then I did a little digging in case you actually showed up."

"I was going to make an appointment after the first of the year."

"Good, I'll be expecting your call. Now, in the meantime, what have you settled on for office space?"

"Ma'am to be quite honest, my partner and I will be working out of my dining room I'd expect for the first year before we can afford some of the redevelopment space that the city offers grants to start-ups like mine to occupy."

"I see you've paid a visit to city hall." She smiled. "Are you familiar with Port City Industries?" She asked.

I nodded, I had done a little research of my own after Arlo had filled me in on as much as he knew about Kay Dandridge and Port City Industries. "Yes, your company is the largest employer in the city, a family owned and run business. You have three locations including the one here in Gates Point and the majority of your work is department of defense contracts for engine components."

Kay smiled and nodded her head. "I knew I liked you."

"Excuse me for asking but if you have contracts with the federal government why do you need a marketing firm?"

"Very smart question," Kay stood up, "Between you and me I might be thinking about expanding outside of federal work, too many eggs in one basket makes me nervous.

I also need some internal marketing materials as well."

I nodded, "I see,"

"Have you contracted with a printer, yet?" Kay asked.

"We haven't made a final decision yet."

"Want a little piece of friendly advice?"

"Absolutely,"

"Don't scrimp on the print contractor. Hackworth's might be a little more expensive, but you get what you pay for there." She paced a little, "Another thing is that I am willing to pay your price, but I also expect a certain level of service."

I nodded, "Of course."

"What I mean is that I will take up a lot of your time and it would be to my advantage to have you close by."

"Okay." I wasn't sure where she was going with this conversation.

She smiled at me then, and I had a feeling the shoe was about to drop, "I own this building. This is corporate headquarters for Port City, and I think I might be able to get you a deal on the rent."

My mouth dropped open, etiquette said I should close it, but I couldn't.

She laughed the kind of laugh that was contagious.

"I appreciate that, but I don't think you understand there is absolutely no way I can afford this building no matter how much of a discount you can talk that gentleman into."

"He works for me or at least I contract with his company, he will be obligated to charge you whatever price I tell him to."

I could see how she became the CEO of a very powerful company. She was used to getting her way.

"Well, there is one more complication. It wouldn't be fair for me to make a decision about our location without consulting my partner."

"Of course, I tell you what. Why don't you hold onto these and bring him back to have a look, then when your down stop by my office and we can have a chat. Anytime on Friday will be fine."

"I don't...,"

Kay held up her hand, "trust me, talk to your partner. Think about it. No pressure, if you still want to work from home, you will still get my business. No harm, no foul." She smiled.

"Okay," I nodded feeling a little more relieved. "I'll do that."

"Okay, well I am going to leave you here for now." She shook my hand again. "I'll see you Friday."

"Yes, ma'am." I stood in the empty space looking around. I walked into each of the offices. Finally, I backed out and locked the door behind me. I pocketed the keys and drove home. I could hardly contain myself. I ran upstairs to stash the gifts then went back downstairs and text Arlo. 'Can you come over now?'

'I'll be right over.'

A moment later there was a knock at the door and Arlo's voice rang out. "Hello? Ginny?"

I poked my head around the corner, "In here!"

"Hey, you left these in the door." He said holding up my house keys.

"Oh gosh, thank you."

"Are you okay?"

"I don't know, I think so."

Arlo looked at me clearly concerned but I think it was more for my sanity than my physical well-being.

I had to laugh he was so serious. "Okay, we better sit down," I pointed to the chairs. Which didn't do anything to calm him. "First, I'm fine. I just had a really weird afternoon and I couldn't wait to get home and tell you about it." Finally, the concern left his face.

"Okay, what happened?"

"I went downtown to do some shopping and by the way you were right that Christmas tree down there is amazing!"

He finally smiled, "I know right?"

"Anyway, I was just sort of looking around and exploring and there was this huge office building and the tree and the ice-skating rink it made me think of New York, you know?"

"You were feeling homesick?"

"Not really, I was just thinking one day I want us to be able to have a nice office like the ones in New York or like the ones I imagined were in the office building I was standing in front of. And I ran into Kay Dandridge again."

"She is going to think you are stalking her or something." Arlo laughed.

I laughed too, "I don't think so. She is really a genuinely nice person. Intense, but nice."

"I've heard that."

"Well anyway, she recognized me and asked if I was looking at leasing space in the building. I explained that we would be working out of the dining room for a while, but she insisted we go in and look at the space anyway just to see what downtown office space looks like and how much it costs. I insisted there was no way I could afford anything in that zip code, but she insisted," I paused, "The offices were beautiful, better than anyplace I ever worked in New York. Long story short, she owns the whole freaking building!"

"What are you telling me, that you want to rent space in this building?"

I could see he was about to protest.

"No, that is not what I am saying. I am saying that she wants us to go look at the space together because I told her I don't do anything without my business partner, and she wants to meet with us on Friday in her office!"

"What? Why?"

"She is hiring us to handle the marketing for her new business expansion and for some internal marketing campaign. She said she would give us the details on Friday." I squealed and bounced up and down in my chair. Arlo being more pragmatic leaned back and ran his hand over his face.

"Are you sure that is what she said?"

"I'm positive."

"Wow!"

"I know! I know! This is better than I ever thought possible. I mean I thought we would be doing flyers for plumbing companies or something. I didn't imagine landing a corporate account before we are even officially open."

"This is a lot to take in."

"You're not mad, are you?"

"Mad? Why would I be mad? It is just a lot to take in. I hadn't planned on having to buy new suits just yet, I only have the one."

"Well, it is a good-looking suit, it will be fine. Oh, and she let me keep the keys to the empty office space so you and I could go look at it on our own." I held up the keys.

"Wow, this is really happening isn't it?"

I was still feeling giddy, "Yeah and really fast too."

"I know we said no business until after Christmas, but I think we better get to it."

"You're right. She also recommended using Hackworth printing, have you heard of them?"

"I know a Doug Hackworth from school, I think his dad might own a printing company, well we might want to go check them out."

"I'll give them a call." Arlo said fishing his cell phone from his pocket.

I looked at the papers on the table and started reviewing the business plan and confirming things I had been working on like the business cards, and our own advertising. I wanted to put together a portfolio and biographies for both Arlo and me. I had purchased a domain name and Arlo was working on the webpage and social media pages. I wanted something online before we met with Kay Dandridge on Friday.

December Fourth

Ginny

Opening the door Friday morning to see Arlo standing there looking incredibly handsome in his suit with a new haircut. Although, I missed his wayward curls. "You look very nice,"

"Thank you. You as well." He nodded to my heather-gray suit and heels, "You ready?"

"I am." I grabbed my purse, keys, and briefcase.

We drove downtown and I found the parking garage close the Port City's Industries building. We approached the security desk inside the Port City's office building.

"My name is Ginny Graham, this is Arlo Michaels, Ms. Dandridge said we could stop by anytime today and look at some empty office space."

The man behind the desk was dressed in a blue blazer and gray pants. He had a military buzzcut and a very serious look. He tapped on the computer. Then looked at Arlo and I and nodded.

"Do you have keys for the office space you want to see?"

"I do, Ms. Dandridge gave them to me."

He nodded, "Ms. Dandridge's office is on the twenty-fifth floor," He said sliding a sign-in sheet over to me. "You can go up when you're ready."

"Thank you," I signed the sheet and slid it over to Arlo.

We made our way to the elevator and I pressed the button for the twelfth floor.

"Wow, he takes his job very seriously." Arlo said once we were alone.

"Yeah, he seemed to." I agreed. "probably a good thing, though."

"I'd feel safe working here with him at the front door."

"No kidding." I agreed.

The doors opened and Arlo let me go first. I led the way to the offices and opened the door. Arlo was looking around taking it all in until he stepped inside the office space.

"Whoa!"

"I know, it's pretty impressive right?"

"You know there is absolutely no way we can afford this, don't you?"

"Yeah, I know. But it is so pretty. I just had to see it one more time."

We walked around looking at the conference room and the view to the street below.

It was nearly eleven thirty, I took a deep breath, "Shall we go up and see Ms. Dandridge?"

Arlo looked nervous. "I guess so."

I nodded and locked the door behind us. We rode the elevator in silence. The doors opened into a lobby on the twenty-fifth floor, there was a reception desk at the end of the room. With smaller hallways branching off to the left and right. We walked straight ahead.

The woman looked up and smiled sweetly. "Can I help you?"

"Virginia Graham here to see Ms. Dandridge."

"Do you have an appointment?"

"No ma'am she said to drop by anytime."

The woman tapped on her keyboard and then looked at Arlo, "Your name, sir?"

"Arlo Michaels."

"Thank you, have a seat."

We sat on the sofa on the opposite wall. I was more nervous than I thought I would be. Arlo was pale.

The receptionist picked up the phone and spoke in low tones. I couldn't hear what she was saying. We waited a few more minutes and the heavy oak door to our right opened and a man with salt and pepper hair trimmed very close stepped out and smiled at us, he left the door open and a moment later Kay Dandridge appeared.

"Ms. Graham, please come in,"

Arlo and I stood and walked into her large office. It was well appointed but plain. It was more function over form.

"Please let's sit at the conference table."

"Thank you, this is my business partner, Arlo Michaels."

"Mr. Michaels it is a pleasure to meet you."

Kay and Arlo shook hands. "Ms. Dandridge, a pleasure." Arlo said with a confidence I hadn't expected.

"Did Ms. Graham show you the office space downstairs?"

"Yes, she did, it is very impressive."

Kay smiled and nodded. "It's a little flashy for my tastes, but it is very comfortable."

"It is very well appointed. It reminds me of New York." I smiled.

"Speaking of New York, tell me more about your work there." Kay said getting down to business.

"I brought my portfolio; I hope you don't mind." I offered.

"That's great," Kay leaned in to look as I slid the book over to her.

I glanced at Arlo, who was looking uncomfortable.

Kay was silent for a few moments and then she closed the book and turned her attention on Arlo,

"Mr. Michaels what is your background?"

Arlo shifted a little in his seat and I held my breath. I knew he was nervous and was having a case of self-doubt. We had talked about it at length and I hoped his nerves wouldn't get the best of him.

"Ma'am my experience isn't in marketing, I do have a business degree and I have been working on a fishing vessel and running my own handy-man business while putting together enough savings to start my own company."

"A fishing boat," Kay considered the words for a moment, "so you are no stranger to hard work."

"No ma'am."

"What made you decide to go into the marketing business with Ms. Graham?"

I was surprised by the question and I'm sure Arlo was too.

"As I mentioned it has always been my intention to start my own business and Ms. Graham and I are neighbors and friends. When she started thinking about whether to stay in Gates Point or return to New York, I suggested she start her own marketing business here. I thought Gates Point would benefit from having her here. But, running the day to day business side of things, is more my area than Ginny's," He nodded to me and smiled. "She is so very creative that her time needs to be spend there and we thought I could handle the nuts and bolts of the operation."

"I see," Kay nodded and sat back in her chair, clearly considering everything we had presented. "I know you have researched my company and so you know my maternal grandfather started it, then my father took it over then my mother briefly before she passed away, also from cancer."

I hadn't heard that, and I felt an instant connection to Kay.

"My grandfather and father both started in this business working with their hands; welders and machinists, they knew the value of hard work, they also believed in giving people a chance and helping others when you had the ability to help." She got up and walked to her desk and retrieved a folder.

"I like what I see in you two, you are helping each other with the abilities you have, and you've been honest, you didn't come up here and give me some bullshit story or try to make yourselves out to be something you are not. I respect that."

I remained silent I felt like she was building up to something.

"I believe in helping people when I am able." She slid a contract over to Arlo and me.

"I have the ability to control the rent in this building, since it is bought and paid for by my grandfather and father. Real estate is a very small branch of this company, but it is one that is nearly pure profit, that being said, I think location is everything in business, do you agree, Mr. Michael?"

"Yes, ma'am."

"Here is a lease agreement for the space downstairs for one year,"

I slid it to Arlo, who began reading and turning pages. He looked up, "This is rent free."

"Yes, it is." Kay smiled.

"But," Arlo started. Kay held up her hand.

"Don't worry there is a catch."

Arlo nodded.

She looked at me, "The catch is I want a contract with you as I mentioned to you before, I need a new marketing campaign and I want you to handle it. I also would feel better knowing you are just downstairs, and I can pop in and talk about my ideas with you."

I was trying very hard not to smile. Arlo remained stoic. Kay continued on,

"Both contracts will be valid for one year at the end of that year we will reevaluate where we are and see if we are both happy with the arrangement or if changes need to be made."

"Seems fair so far." Arlo added.

Kay smiled, "A true businessman, yes, we will discuss your fee."

Arlo opened his portfolio and produced the standard contract we had developed, "Would now be a good time to talk particulars?"

"Absolutely,"

Arlo passed the contract over to Kay and winked at me. I smiled back. We waited while Kay read it over.

"This sounds fair," She took out a pen and signed it then handed it back to Arlo. Arlo looked it over and signed it.

"If you like I can have Sherry make a copy of that before you leave."

"Yes, that would be very nice." Arlo smiled for the first time.

Kay stood up, "Well, looks like we have a deal." She held out her hand to me and Arlo.

We followed her to the door.

"Sherry can you make a copy of this contract and give the original back to Mr. Michaels and Ms. Graham?"

"Of course,"

Kay turned back to us, "Keep the keys to the office, I've arranged for the furniture to stay until you are ready to replace it. Let the real estate office know of anything you need. They can help you get set up with telephone and internet service."

"Thank you very much," I said shaking her hand again.

"My pleasure. I can't wait to see what you come up with for the marketing campaign. I'll email you some ideas and maybe we can meet after the first of the year to see what you have for me?"

"Yes ma'am." I was having a hard time containing my enthusiasm.

Arlo and I left; we didn't say anything at all until we were back at my house. Once inside with the door closed. I turned to him and smiled the biggest smile. "We did it!"

"Hell yes, we did!" Now he smiled and scooped me up in a hug and swung me around. "We did it!"

He put me back down on the floor and kissed me.

I froze. It wasn't a passionate kiss, but it was a kiss on the lips and my heart felt like it was going to beat out of my chest. Arlo sensed my shock and pulled back.

"Sorry," his cheeks reddened.

"Don't be! We did good today!" I recovered quickly, not knowing if the kiss had felt the same for him.

December Seventh

Arlo

I slept later than I had in years. My body was starting to get used to not having to be up at three in the morning. I had been staying up later as a result. I didn't mind rising with the sun at all it felt good. Today, I would make breakfast on my hot plate and dress to move a few boxes to the new office space. I was still trying to wrap my head around the events of yesterday and I was still a little wary of our sudden good luck. But I also wasn't about to look a gift horse in the mouth as they say.

Ginny and I had signed a very lucrative contract with Port City Industries for a one-year campaign and as part of the deal we got office space in the best building downtown for free, it was too good to be true. There had to be another catch. I didn't know a lot about Kay Dandridge, but what I did know was that she was a good businesswoman, she was fair, and everyone who worked for Port City Industries enjoyed it. I was going to have to ask around a little more. Still at the moment everything seemed to be going our way, it had been a risk to quit my job and start a business from scratch and even though Port City was a big client it was a small project, and we couldn't live off one or two clients even if we did have an office rent free. Monday I was going to look into joining the local chamber of commerce and maybe looking into a better apartment in the near future. Something with a little more room in it. And then there was the kiss. I don't know why I did it. But it just seemed like the thing to do at the time. It felt right even after. The look of shock on Ginny's face told me she hadn't been expecting anything like that at all. What had I been thinking? There had never been any flirting between us. Nothing even remotely close to romantic. We were friends, really good friends and now business partners. There was no reason to think Ginny was focused on anything else and I was a complete idiot for what I had done. The question was now, how did Ginny feel about it? Was it going to be weird today? Had I ruined things before they got started? Should I apologize for it? I wasn't sorry I did it, frankly I'd do it again if I thought she was into it.

I decided I wouldn't bring it up if she didn't. With that final thought, I closed my apartment door and headed across the street. I needed to think about getting a car soon too. I couldn't expect Ginny to drive me to and from work and if I was going out to drum up business, I couldn't do it on a bicycle.

"Hey good morning," Ginny smiled as she opened the door and invited me in.

"Hey,"

"I've got everything boxed up; we just need to get them out to the car."

"I would have helped you."

"I know, but I was too keyed up to sleep last night, so I just went ahead and did it."

I shook my head, typical Ginny.

"Did you sleep at all?" I asked lifting a box and heading to the door.

"Yeah a little but honestly not much. What about you?"

"Slept like a baby." I smiled.

She laughed, that wonderful infectious laugh that she had. It was light and not too loud, but one that made you want to laugh right along with her. "So, what's the plan for today?"

"Well," She said opening the trunk of the car, "I thought we would see about getting the office set up and taking an inventory of what we needed, then we can go shopping downtown, I'm sure there is an office supply store around there somewhere and we can grab a few things, any high-ticket items we can check online for better deals."

"Sounds like a plan."

I loved watching her when she was passionate about something. I was regretting the kiss less and less.

We drove downtown and parked in the loading dock long enough to get the boxes out of the car and then we hauled them upstairs via a service elevator. I have to admit I was impressed with the help we got from the building services staff and security, I was a little less skeptical about the arrangement, it seemed more legit today. The building staff offered to move furniture around for us if we wanted it, but we opted for a 'wait and see' approach.

There was a man already adding our names to the door and he said he would add our names to the lobby directory as well.

It was starting to feel more real to me and I had the urge to hug Ginny again, but I controlled myself.

Ginny

Arlo and I spent the next week and half working our tails off at the office, getting phone and internet connections made, we bought computers and supplies. I put out feelers for part time reception help with Wendy and Becca. Arlo even bought himself a new car. He had made a few contacts through the Chamber of Commerce network meetings he had attended, and it looked like we were going to be able to start strong. I spent time working on designs and ideas for Port City, I wanted to make sure we had a couple of different options for our January deadline with Kay. Arlo and I were spending a lot more time together and, in some ways, I wished we worked from home instead of the office, we often left late and recently in separate cars. I missed riding to work with him. I hadn't mentioned the kiss and neither had Arlo, but it was still on my mind and I wondered if he was thinking about it too. My skin tingled each time our hands touched when looking over documents with one another or setting up the computers. Even now remembering each of those moments I got a warm feeling in the pit of my stomach. Each time it happened I tried to peak at Arlo nonchalantly, but he was always stone faced.

I was working in my office on a design, when I heard Arlo talking with someone in the outer office. A moment later he was standing in my doorway, wearing a suit that must have been new, I didn't recognize it.

"Hey look, a Christmas reception." He was holding up a flyer.

Christmas, I had forgotten all about Christmas, in the rush to get some designs together and moving into the office. Which was my original plan, it just seemed to have worked better than I expected. "Really?"

"Yeah, apparently it will be downstairs in the lobby for all of the buildings tenants." He looked excited. I felt the pit of my stomach churn.

"I bet Kay is paying for it." I tried to smile.

"You're probably right, well it is at five o'clock on the 18th."

"Okay," I forced a smile. But I knew by now Arlo would tell when I was faking it. I didn't have any interest in a Christmas party, and it was only by the grace of god that Wendy hadn't shown up on my doorstep with a party in tow.

I turned back to my screen and plunged back into my work. It was nearing seven o'clock before Arlo reappeared.

"Ginny, I'm going to call it a night."

"Okay, see you tomorrow."

"Ginny come with me, let's go to dinner you need a break."

I looked up; he was so sweet. "I'm okay."

"You need to eat, you didn't take lunch, come on, you can come back and work all night if you want, just come to dinner with me."

He did have a point. I was hungry and the yogurt at lunch had worn off long ago.

"Okay, I suppose food is a good idea."

He smiled. Arlo had always been good looking but with the new haircut and clothes, he was magazine cover material.

"Where too?" Once we were outside in the cold, the wind cut right through my coat and I hoped wherever we were going was close by.

"Well, there is a nice steak house down this way," he pointed.

"Okay, lead on." I pulled my coat close in around me. "I swear I don't see how it couldn't possibly snow for Christmas."

Arlo laughed, "Oh gets cold but it's too cold to snow."

"That doesn't even make sense."

"Sure, it does," He laughed. "We never get snow at Christmas, it will come later, we might get a Nor'easter though and that will bring lots of ice and the power will be out for days."

"Great sounds like fun."

"It can be." He looked down at me for a brief moment.

Was he flirting with me? He looked away quickly. "Well, good if it goes out, I'll have you come over and help me bring firewood in."

He laughed, "I'll be there."

The restaurant was cozy and warm. It had a tavern feel to it with exposed beams in the ceiling and warm polished wooden booths.

"If you are in the mood for seafood, they get theirs locally from the docks." Arlo advised.

"Okay," I nodded and scanned the menu. I went for a grilled chicken salad just the same. I realized Arlo must know quite a bit about what restaurants sourced locally. "Arlo, you know a lot of the restaurants in town and where they get their food, why didn't you go into the restaurant business?"

He looked at me and smirked. "I was tired of coming home smelling like fish, a restaurant business isn't far enough removed from that life."

I laughed, "Point taken."

"Besides, I like not having to get up at three in the morning." He gave me a devilish grin.

"I understand that. I don't envy anyone that has to keep those kinds of hours."

We finished our meal and I went home. While we had an office, I still worked from home at night. I was often more creative after the sun went down and nothing beat working in a fuzzy pair of warm socks and a sweatshirt. I wanted to work on a campaign I had in mind for Wendy and planned to stop by the shop tomorrow and show it to her.

December Eighth

Ginny

I left work early to drive over to Bumboat Books, the store had quite a few customers when I walked in. I had never seen the place so busy, Becca was at the register and Wendy was helping a customer find a book.

"Hi Becca,"

"Oh Ginny, so good to see you!"

"Need any help?" I asked seeing people forming a line.

"Would you, really?" She looked desperate.

I laughed, "Sure!" I put my things down in the back and hurried back up front. I pulled out the mobile credit card scanner and started helping people in the line. After about thirty minutes the shop had cleared.

Wendy put her arm around me. "Whew! Thank you so much Ginny!"

"I'm glad I was here to help, that was crazy, has it been like that a lot?"

"Yeah, those coupons we mailed have been flying through the door. This is going to be our best year yet." Wendy smiled.

"I'm so glad. And I have something to show you that I think you might like."

"Okay." Wendy and I walked to the back and sat down at the worktable while I went over my presentation of a whole year of promotions based on holidays, some obscure others more celebrated like Valentine's Day.

"These look wonderful Ginny!"

"I'm so glad you like them."

"How is it going?"

"It's going great, we have a wonderful office downtown, Arlo is really a natural at running things, so I get to spend my time creating."

Wendy hugged me. "I am so happy for you!"

"Thank you, it is a little hard to believe still. I keep pinching myself." I laughed.

"Do you have a lot of clients?"

"Not yet, we have a one-year contract with Port City Industries, that is a really big account and I have a presentation to make to them after the first of the year."

"Wow, I am just so happy for you, now what are you doing for Christmas?"

I had been dreading this question, but I was also prepared for it.

"I have dinner plans with Arlo."

"With Arlo, really?"

"Yeah, he can't go see his folks this year in Florida so I thought I would treat him to a Christmas dinner."

"You know you are welcome at our place."

"I know and I appreciate that, but I think a nice relaxing Christmas at home is what I need."

Wendy eyed me suspiciously, but she didn't press.

I stayed and chatted a while longer and then drove home. I suddenly had a different perspective on the holidays, telling Wendy about the new business made me realize how lucky I really was and that my mother would be proud of me.

I went home and started going through the decorations that Arlo had been kind enough to pull down from the attic and I hadn't bothered to unpack. I put on some Christmas music; poured myself a glass of wine and started decorating on room at a time. By one in the morning, I was getting tired and I decided to save the other rooms for later. But at least most of the downstairs was decorated with the exception of the tree. I hadn't been able to bring myself to that task just yet.

Arlo

The days were passing quickly and there was so much to be done to prepare our presentation to Kay Dandridge and then Christmas dinner with Ginny was fast approaching. I wasn't sure which made me more nervous. I went down to the docks and reserved some oysters, scallops, crab and flounder for the Christmas dinner I promised to cook for Ginny. I wanted it to be nice, but I was afraid a traditional meal might bring back too many memories for her and I knew she was working really hard not to let the memories of Christmas past weigh on her. She missed her mother and was throwing herself into her work to try and cope with the loss.

Tomorrow we had interviews for a part time office assistant. I had been putting off apartment hunting until after the first of the year. I stepped outside for a breath of fresh air. I saw the lights on across the street and as I walked closer like a moth to a flame, I could hear Christmas music.

I smiled to myself. I wondered what she was wearing and if she would welcome some company. Part of me said turn around and let her have her ritual, another part of me said go knock on the door and see if she needs help. Nothing risked is nothing gained.

I took a deep breath and walked up on the porch. I knocked rather than ring the bell thinking if she didn't hear the knock of the music then I was a complete coward, but I also had risked embarrassing myself.

The door opened.

"Hi," she said standing there in an oversized sweatshirt, a pair of sweatpants and outrageous fuzzy red socks. I had to smile.

"Hi, I, uh," I was starting to lose my nerve. "I saw the lights on and heard music."

"Come on in."

She wobbled a little as she stepped aside and I could tell that she had been drinking, I'm sure it wasn't much two glasses of wine usually made her silly. And I thought about her tradition with her mom when they decorated and drank wine and my heart squeezed tight for her trying to continue the tradition alone. She was too young for that sort of thing.

"I hope I'm not intruding." I offered.

"Not all, can I get you anything, wine? Beer?"

"Beer."

She bounced into the kitchen.

"I was just about to quit for the night, come tell me what you think so far,"

She took my hand and led me into the living room first. It was like a Christmas wonderland and I had seen them all before when I used to help her mother pull them out and pack them away. But I didn't want to rain on her parade.

"Wow, you've done a great job, this is like the north pole."

She looked at me a little unfocused and smiled. "You think so?"

"Yeah, I do."

She squeezed my hand and that made the lie worth it. While it was lovely, the decorations somehow didn't seem to fit Ginny's style. I thought of her as more of a minimalist than an over the top everything in red and white. Next we went into the dining room where there was a white tablecloth, a red table runner and candles and greenery. The greenery was artificial, but her mother used to get fresh and intermix them together to achieve the smell without all the messy clean-up she used to say.

"I noticed you haven't put the tree up yet."

She looked at me and something flashed across her face, was it anger? Sadness? It was gone too quick for me to be able to tell.

"No,"

I felt bold in that moment. "Do you want some help or are you going to skip the tree this year."

She stood there looking at me for a moment I thought she might ask me to leave. Instead she started to cry. I kicked myself for being such a fool.

"Ginny, I'm so sorry. I'm an idiot." I went to her and put my arms around her not knowing really what else to do.

She collapsed into my arms and sobbed on my shoulder, like she had been holding it in for quite some time. I stroked her hair and made soothing noises. When it was obvious this was going to last for a little while, I bent down and scooped her up and carried her into the den and sat down on the sofa.

"I.Sorry." she hiccupped.

"Don't be, let it all out." I continued to stroke her hair and then made small circles on her back.

Finally, she cried herself out and slowly sat up.

"God, I'm so embarrassed." She sniffled.

"Why, because you have feelings? Because you miss your mom. Don't be embarrassed." I whispered.

"I bet I look just lovely," She struggled to get up. I lifted her out of my lap. "I'll be right back."

She headed up stairs to her bathroom. I sat on the sofa and chided myself while I waited for her to return. After several minutes I wondered if I shouldn't just show myself out. I drained what was left of my beer and took it to the kitchen to rinse it and put it in the recycle bin when she met me at the doorway. She had washed her face, her eyes were a little less red. She had brushed her hair, and she was gorgeous in the sweats and big fuzzy socks.

"You okay?" I asked.

"Yes, I know I keep saying it, but I am sorry I broke down on you like that."

"I understand, I'm glad I was here for you." I took a risk and stepped closer. She let me hug her. She wrapped her arms tight about me.

"You've been here for me through all of this, quietly helping me out and rescuing me. I'm sure I've been just awful."

"You've been under a lot of stress and rightfully so. You never have to apologize to me." I said taking a step back and looking down into her soft eyes. I let my finger run along her jaw line. "I'll always be here for you, no matter what." Her smile warmed me to my core, and I started to feel warm in a few other places. I fought the urge to kiss her. She must have sensed and pulled back a little.

"I should go,"

"Okay," she nodded hesitantly, and I wondered if I should offer to stay a little longer.

"We have those interviews tomorrow."

"Oh yeah, right." She bit her lower lip and it shot arrows through my heart.

I stepped past her and headed for the door. I thought about going home to my tiny apartment, I thought about seeing her at work the next day, I thought about all the days going forward that we would continue this dance of being only friends and not admitting we wanted more.

I opened the door and stepped out onto the porch. I turned back to face her.

"Good night, and remember I am just across the street if you need me."

She nodded and smiled; her lips pressed together.

I got to the bottom of the stairs. I hated my apartment, but I couldn't imagine living somewhere that would take me further away from Ginny.

I heard the door close softly behind me.

December Twenty-Fourth

Ginny

We closed the office for Christmas Eve, not that we were officially open yet, but Arlo and I agreed not to go to work that day. My cell phone rang at ten o'clock.

"Hello?"

"Hey, its me." Arlo's voice made me smile.

"Hey you."

"I wanted to see if you were awake yet and if you felt like having some company."

"I'm up and dressed, you are welcome to come over any time." I knew he must be missing his family this year and frankly I wasn't looking forward to spending the day alone.

Twenty minutes later there was a knock at the door, I called out for Arlo to come in. He had taken to knocking rather than ringing the bell, so I knew it was him.

"Good morning, I brought donuts!" Arlo called as he came through the door. A man after my own heart when it came to food. Despite the business lunches and the pizza and beer nights he had managed to stay in perfect shape. Now that he wasn't working on the boat anymore, he had taken up jogging and cycling. I on the other hand had gained five pounds. I was going to be a cliché this year and have a new year's resolution to get into shape.

"I see you still haven't put up a tree," he said lightly.

We had been avoiding that conversation for a couple of weeks now since my crying jag.

"Yeah, well you know." I tried to shrug it off.

"Well, I thought maybe you'd like a new Christmas tree tradition."

"Okay, I'm listening." I was a little suspicious.

"I thought maybe you'd like a short drive to the country, and we could chop down a live tree for you."

"What? A real tree, where are we going to get a real tree?"

"A friend of mine owns quite a bit of property not far from here and he said we can come over and look for a tree if we find one, we can have it."

"Really?" I had to admit the idea was exciting.

"You might want to put on some warmer clothes though." He grinned.

"Is it really that cold out there?

"Yes, and where we are going it is likely to be colder."

I ran upstairs and changed into heavy jeans, boots and a flannel shirt. When I came down the stairs Arlo laughed.

"You look like a regular lumberjack."

"Hush up!" I fussed.

I grabbed a coat, hat, gloves and scarf and followed him out the door.

Arlo drove us out of Gates Point north, crossing over the York river. The sky was steel gray, and the clouds were heavy. I know snow clouds when I see them despite Arlo's insistence that we would not get snow for Christmas. We drove until I was sure we were leaving Gloucester County, but then Arlo slowed and turned off of route seventeen. We took another turn and stopped at a heavy metal gate. Arlo got out and unlocked the gate pushing it opened and drove through. He closed it behind us, and we followed a dirt road through the trees until we came to a little house.

"The hunting lodge?" I asked seeing the small frame house with a front porch. It was plain but well maintained.

"Yes," He smiled. There were no other cars around, so I assumed we had the place to ourselves.

"No one should be here hunting today but put this on just in case." He handed me a blaze orange vest.

"What's this for?"

"I don't want anyone mistaking you for a deer.

"Me either."

Arlo went to the trunk and removed a small chain saw and an axe. "Well, let's go find a tree."

"Lead the way."

We followed a trail of sorts for a while and started to investigate any evergreen we saw growing. We had been walking for nearly two hours when I finally spotted it.

"There, look at that one!"

Arlo walked ahead pushing limbs out of the way, "Yes, this looks like a good one."

"You don't think it is too tall?" I asked.

"No, I think it will be perfect."

Just then a tiny, very wet snowflake fell on my nose. "Oh!"

"What is it?"

I looked up at the sky, the tree branches spread out in a black maze against the heavy clouds. Then Arlo saw it too,

"Snow!" I announced with a 'I told you so' attitude.

"So it is." Arlo held out a gloved hand and watched as a few more flakes landed there. "We better get to work if we want to get out of here before this starts accumulating."

"Okay, tell me what to do."

"Stand over there out of the way." He pointed. He revved up the chainsaw and a moment later the tree was down. "Okay, now we just have to drag it back to the car.

"Let me carry something."

"Here take the chainsaw and axe but be careful."

I did as he instructed, fortunately it only took about forty-five minutes to get back to the car but by then it was snowing in earnest. Arlo grabbed a moving blanket, and some rope out of the trunk and we lifted the tree onto the blanket spread across the roof of his car. I got in and turned on the heat while he lashed the tree down.

Arlo hopped in the car and took off his gloves and rubbing his hands together. "Ready to go home?"

I nodded, "Ready."

We drove home and I fully expected the snow to stop once we crossed the York River, but it didn't, the clouds seemed to be following us.

"It looks like you might get your wish for a white Christmas." Arlo said studying the sky as we got closer and closer to the water.

I giggled at the thought.

We used the blanket to get the tree into the house and avoid dropping too many needles and small branches. I retrieved the tree stand from one of the boxes and an empty coffee can from the recycling bin to put some water in it for the tree. Within minutes I had a beautiful spruce standing in the den in front of the windows.

"That is almost pretty enough without decorations." I said admiring our handywork.

Arlo crossed his arms over his chest proudly. "Well, a few ornaments or maybe some tinsel couldn't hurt."

"How about some hot cocoa?"

"Perfect, you get the cocoa, I'll go get the ornaments." I watched him leave and thought about how lucky I was to have a friend like Arlo and how tempting it was to allow myself to feel more for him.

"Okay, so let's see what we have here." He smiled sitting the box down in front of the tree. "Lights first I think, do you want all white or different colored lights?"

I handed him a mug of cocoa, "I think all white."

"Good choice." He fished the lights of the box. They were neatly wound around a piece of cardboard to keep them from getting tangled. I should have known. He began stringing the lights. I stood sipping the cocoa and watching him allowing my mind to wonder to places it shouldn't go. Once he was done, he plugged them in, and the tree lit up.

"How's that?"

I laughed with joy. "Perfect!"

"Okay, now for the ornaments, they are divided up by type. So, I have what appear to be childhood favorites in this box," He pointed, "this box are pewter and silver ornaments, and that box is baubles."

"Baubles?"

"Yeah, glass ornaments that are either balls or some other shape, some look very old"

"What they aren't color coded?" I teased.

"Hmm, he rubbed his five o'clock shadow, well we can certainly do that when we pack them away this year."

"I liked it when he said 'we' I knew he only said because he was used to doing this for my mother every year. But it still had a nice ring to it.

"I think we should keep it simple and just do the metal ornaments." I walked over and picked up one and removed it from its soft protective bag. It was a pewter stag with a red ribbon attached. I walked over and placed it on the tree. "Now it is your turn."

Arlo nodded and selected an ornament and hung it on the tree.

"Aren't we missing some music?" he asked.

"Yes! I turned on the Bluetooth speaker and found my Christmas playlist on my phone.

The scene was perfect, Arlo hanging ornaments, music, a tree we cut ourselves and the snow falling outside was visible in the background of my little Christmas scene through the window. It was like my own personal snow globe.

We spent the next hour laughing and singing while decorating the tree.

Once we were done, I turned off the lights in the room.

"The tree is so beautiful." I whispered. "Thank you." I could feel Arlo's eyes on me, and I turned to him. He was staring down at me, a small smile playing at the corner of his lips.

"You deserve everything beautiful in the world."

I blinked and thought I had misheard him. But then he cupped my face and leaned in and pressed his warm lips to mine. My mind was spinning as I tried to grasp what was happening. I returned his kiss and felt his other hand in the middle of my back pulling me closer to him. My mind was screaming a thousand reasons why this was a very bad idea. First and foremost, we were business partners and friends. How would this change that relationship? But my body didn't seem to be getting the message because it was responding to Arlo all on its own. I wrapped my arms around his neck and accepted a passionate kiss. I was strangely aware of the song that was playing at that moment. The scent of cocoa mixed with his aftershave, the feeling of his five o'clock shadow on my chin. The heat radiating from his hands that were strong yet gentle.

"Arlo," I whispered against his lips.

He pulled away and looked down at me, "Are you okay?"

I nodded.

"Are you okay with this?" He asked putting his lips close to my ear.

"Hmm, hmm," The warmth of his breath making me forget how to speak for a moment. He began nuzzling my neck and my knees started to go weak. I gripped him to keep from sinking to the floor. He felt my knees buckling and he guided me slowly down in front of the tree. I framed his face with my hands and admired the lines of his face in the glow of the soft white lights. The warmth of his brown eyes were like deep pools as he stared down at me and smiled. My heart skipped a beat or was it two?

He kissed me again and this time I was ready for it and I matched his passion. When we finally came up for air, his lips were still close to mine.

"Do you know how long I have wanted to do that?"

"Really?"

"From the moment I met you."

I smiled against his cheek. "I'm glad you did it." I don't know if he heard me, he was busy kissing my neck and making me think of all sorts of wicked things he could be doing with those lips. But I wasn't sure I was ready to take things all the way just yet.

Arlo

I had made arrangements with my friend, Bob, to take Ginny out to his property to look for a Christmas tree. Bob was sympathetic to how Ginny was feeling about the holidays and was more than happy to give away one tree amongst hundreds on his thirty acres. I had hoped that this trip and the tree would be a different kind of Christmas gift for Ginny, that returned the Christmas spirit to her heart without replacing all those wonderful Christmas memories she was holding on to so tightly. Ginny had been more agreeable to the plan than I had thought she would be. I was prepared for more of an argument and once we were in the woods, she seemed to be transformed. She was alive again with a glow in her eyes that hadn't been there since her mother's funeral. And when it started snowing her heart seemed to be set free. The look on her face, the smile that reached her eyes when that first snowflake fell was something that filled my heart with joy. I was surprised to see so much snow falling so fast and I was sure it wouldn't last; the flakes were heavy and wet a sure sign that it would be pretty for a while but would soon be gone. She was giddy as a schoolgirl when we got home, and it was still snowing. The flakes were smaller by the bay and I had a feeling she might get her wish for a white Christmas after all. I had been struggling with my feelings for her and it was getting harder and harder to keep them in check. But, tonight, with the snow and decorating the tree together, I knew my heart would explode if I didn't at least kiss her. I knew I was risking everything; she might slap my face. It might put a strain on our professional relationship, and I was being selfish not to care about any of that, I knew I had to taste her lips. I had to know that they were as warm and soft as I imagined them. I needed to know if I was following a fool's dream.

To my surprise when I stepped in close and kissed her lightly, she didn't run away or kick me out of the house. And she was as warm and tasted sweet like honey and hot cocoa. And when she returned my kiss my heart soared into the heavens. I could spend the rest of my life just kissing Ginny Graham. I wished I had laid a fire in the fireplace; it would have been perfect to lay her down in front of the fire and make love to her. But that would have to wait. I was more of a gentleman than that and I knew she had a higher moral code, but at that moment with the scent of her hair and the softness of her skin, it was everything I could do, not to unbutton that flannel shirt she was wearing.

The clock on the mantel chimed and I rested next to her on my elbow. She rolled onto her side to face me. She stared deep into my eyes, as if she was searching for something. She began tracing my jawline with her index finger and I felt like I was in heaven.

"You are full of surprises, Arlo Michaels."

"So are you, Ginny Graham." And I meant it. I never would have imagined a woman like Ginny could exist. She had taught me to believe in myself and instilled a level of self confidence in me that I would have not thought possible just a few months ago. Her confidence in me and my idea for starting up the marketing business gave me the confidence to believe in myself and it was that confidence that allowed me the courage to kiss her and show her how I felt about her.

"You're a very special woman, Ginny."

She blushed. Before she could protest, I leaned in and kissed her then getting to my feet and helping her up.

"I should go,"

The look on her face told me she didn't want the night to end any more than I did, but there was a hint of relief there too.

"I'll see you for dinner?" I whispered in her ear.

She bit her lip and nodded. "Okay,"

I let my hand rest on her shoulder for just a moment while I tried to get my feet to move and walk out the front door. "I'll see you in a few hours."

I held her hand while I walked to the door. I could see she was struggle within herself as much as I was, neither of us wanted it to end, but neither of us was ready to take the next step.

I kissed her one last time in the open doorway and stepped off the porch and into the snow. I spread my arms out wide and looked up at the sky.

"Looks like you are getting your wish."

"Yes, it does." She said without taking her eyes off of me and it made me think she wasn't talking about the snow. I turned and walked home.

December Twenty-Fifth

Ginny

I woke up early, like I did every Christmas morning since I was a child. I knew there was no point in going downstairs. There would be no gifts left by Santa, my mother wouldn't be in the kitchen making pancakes.

I laid there thinking about Arlo and the warmth of his hands were and how soft and gentle his lips were against mine. I had been surprised by his kiss, but I was glad I wasn't the only one who felt the way I did. We had both struggled with stopping things last night before we went too far. But, laying here in bed now, I wasn't so sure that it wouldn't be such a bad thing to go to bed with Arlo. Yes, we weren't dating, but there were no rules for the heart. When you knew something was right, that is all that mattered, and I knew in my bones that Arlo Michaels was my soul mate, and I would never care to be with another man. Not that I had a lot of experience in that area. In the years I worked in New York there just wasn't time for a relationship. I worked long hours and didn't have time to meet a lot of people, the few guys I had gone out with had never lasted beyond two or three dates. They had all been nice guys, but I just never clicked with anyone romantically. I stretched and smiled. I was happy to be spending my Christmas with Arlo. I got up and ran myself a nice hot bath and added some scented oils. I would spend the morning pampering myself. It was Christmas after all. When the water started to chill, I got out and decided to resist the urge to dress in something ultra-comfy like yoga pants and an ugly sweater, but instead to dress up and wear something festive. I selected a cream-colored pair of light wool slacks and a green velvet top with matching green velvet flats. I added small pearl earrings.

Thirty minutes later there was a knock at the door, I smiled and embarrassed by the spark in the pit of my stomach. Arlo was here.

I bounced down the stairs and opened the door. "Hello," I was nearly breathless with excitement.

"Uh, hi." He stood staring at me. "You look gorgeous."

I smiled and blushed a little. "You look quite handsome, as well." He did in a pair of gray dress pants, and a burgundy sweater.

"Do come in." I quickly stepped aside.

"I'm not too early, am I?"

"No, of course, not." I wanted to kiss him hello. But, wasn't sure if I should and then I panicked and wondered if he regretted last night.

He looked past me to the tree. "You don't have the tree lit?"

"I haven't been downstairs until just now."

"Oh, so you haven't had coffee yet?"

Seeing the look on his face, I had to ask, "no why?"

"Well normally, you're not this chipper without at least one full cup of coffee."

"Well, I guess I had a reason to get up this morning."

He smiled and leaned in and kissed me lightly. "Me too."

I sighed in relief, no regrets.

He pulled back. "Well, dinner isn't going to cook itself, so I'd better get started."

"Okay, if you must." I was half teasing and half regretting he wasn't prepared to repeat last night right here in the foyer.

I followed him to the kitchen.

"May I borrow your apron?"

"Sure," I grabbed it from the pantry.

He went to the fridge and started grabbing the brown bags of food he had stored there and made me promise not to peak. I had kept my promise, I had no idea what he had in store for today. But it was going to be hard to beat our tree adventure and romantic evening.

I looked out the window to see the snow had stopped falling and there was at least two inches of snow on the ground. I turned to smile at him.

"Yes, I noticed on the way over that you got your wish for a white Christmas."

"Maybe after dinner we can go out for a walk in the snow?" I said like a child begging to be allowed out to build a snowman or go sledding.

"Absolutely," He gave me a sweet kiss on the forehead, "now I am going to need you to have a seat right over here." He said pulling out a kitchen chair for me to sit in. "I will make us some coffee and start the dinner."

"Can I help?"

"No,"

"Okay, then."

We talked about the business, and potential clients, what my ideas were for Port City, what the possibilities were for future contracts with them. The kitchen was steaming, and aromas of spices were floating in the air. I sat the dining room table with the fine china. Finally, Arlo announced dinner was ready.

We started with back river shrimp cocktail, followed by a salad, then flounder stuff with crab, garnished with asparagus and topped with hollandaise sauce. Both, the flounder and crab were locally caught. The rest of the asparagus was roasted with wild mushrooms. And for dessert he had bought a raspberry cheesecake.

"Arlo, that was the most delicious meal I have ever had. I think you missed your calling as a chef."

"No, they have terrible hours, besides it is only fun if I get to do it on my terms."

"Well, that is better than anything I have ever had in a restaurant."

"Good, I'm glad you liked it."

"Let me clean up since you cooked."

"No, we can clean up together."

Arlo was a neat cook and there wasn't a lot of work to be done in the kitchen to clear things up.

"Shall we go into the den and admire our tree?" I suggested.

"Sure,"

He sat on the sofa. I took the Christmas stocking down from the mantel. "This is for you."

"What?" I thought that was just for decoration."

"No, I bought the stocking from a vendor at the lighted boat parade and then I just added a few little things to it."

He looked at me and frowned a little then pulled out the first small package I had wrapped, a pair of monogrammed cufflinks, then the business card holder, and the necktie.

"Ginny, you didn't have to do all of this." He said admiring each one.

"I wanted to; I hope they are okay."

"They are perfect, just like you." He said with a smile. "I can't believe you did all of this, and all I got you was this. He produced a slender box from his pocket.

I was truly surprised I didn't expect a gift from him. I started shaking my head.

"No, Arlo. You've already done so much."

"I haven't done anything."

"The tree, dinner," I waved my arms.

He pulled me close, placing the box in my hands and gently pushing them close to my chest. "those were just something I wanted to do for you."

I kissed him warmly, then whispered, "Thank you,"

"Open it," he whispered back.

I opened the black box to find a beautiful gold bracelet inside.

"Oh Arlo! Its beautiful."

He smiled, "I'm glad you like it."

I took it out of the box and held it up. It was gorgeous, the links not too delicate but not too heavy.

"Here let me help you." He took it and I held out my wrist. He closed the clasp and then bent his head down and kissed the exposed underside of my wrist. It was a simple yet sensual kiss. "Now what do you say we go for that walk and get nice and cold, so we can come back and get warm next to a fire?"

As much as I hated to break the magic of this moment. I liked his idea. A walk in the snow was just too tempting.

"Okay."

Arlo

We dressed in our coats and Ginny changed into a sturdy pair of winter boots. And we walked down to the water's edge. The snow was no match for the saltwater which lapped against the shore. We continued to the seawall and towards the restaurants and shops. Most of which were closed but one or two of the clubs were opening up for evening entertainment and the sounds of a jazz band could be heard.

"Wanna check it out?" I offered.

"Why not?"

We went inside and the band was just warming up.

"Can I get you folks something?"

"Irish coffee, for me." I answered, "And she would like a peppermint hot chocolate." I smiled at Ginny proud of myself for remembering her favorite holiday drink.

We took a seat at a small table and for about thirty minutes we had the place to ourselves and our own private concert. Then as if there was an appointed time, people started to come in, in droves.

I paid the bill, and offered my hand to Ginny, "Shall we?"

She smiled, "Yes,"

We left hand and hand and walked back home. "I'll get the fire started I offered."

"Would you like something else to drink?"

"Whatever you are having."

I watched as she slipped off her boots and padded into the kitchen, she was back a moment later with two glasses of red wine.

She pushed the coffee table out of the way, and we sat on the floor with our backs against the sofa and our feet stretched out towards the fire.

"Arlo, thank you for making this a Christmas to remember."

"You're welcome."

We sipped the wine, until I was sure that I wouldn't be out of place if I decided to kiss her.

"Ginny," I leaned in close until my lips touched her ear. "I am in love with you." I felt her smile.

She turned her face to me and kissed me deeply showing me that she felt the same way.

We kissed until it was no longer enough. I whispered her name.

She could hear the need in my voice and began to run her hands under my sweater, across my back and as I lifted myself up to look into her eyes, she moved her hands to my chest. Then she pulled the sweater over my head. I felt both exposed and at home with her. Her eyes traveled over my chest along with her hands. I tentatively touched her stomach through her blouse, and she nodded. I slipped my hand under and felt her soft flat stomach. My breath caught in my throat and I started to tremble. She scooted back and sat up enough that she lifted her top off. My mouth went dry as I stared at her beauty. Then slowly, I reached for her bra clasp. She gave me a coquettish smile and I unclasp the bra and she let it fall away. My hand was trembling as I touched her again.

We spend the next few hours exploring each other, until both of us were strung as tight as a bow string with needing. The fire was dying, and I stood and wrapped her in the afghan from the sofa and carried her upstairs to her bedroom. I sat her on the edge of the bed and began exploring how to best remove her slacks, I was pleasantly surprised to find she was wearing stockings underneath and I took pleasure in unfastening them and slowly sliding them down each slender leg. Finally, she lay across the bed before me naked, she reached for me, but I made her wait long enough for me to remove my shoes, socks and pants. We spent the next several hours bringing each other to unimaginable heights of love and pleasure. I fell asleep with cradling her in my arms, a changed man.

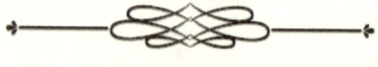

Ginny

I awoke sometime in the middle of the night, my body a little sore but renewed with a different kind of energy and satisfaction. I lay there for a moment wondering if it had all been a wonderful dream and then I felt Arlo's lean body stir next to me. I smiled to myself and reached out for him. At my touch he rolled over and wrapped his arms around me. I laid there knowing everything would be alright in the world wrapped in Arlo's protective cocoon.

The End

Gates Point Series

About the Author

Lynn is a native of the Hampton Roads area of Virginia, the area which is the inspiration for the Gates Point series. She enjoys time in, on and around the Chesapeake Bay and its tributaries. When she isn't out exploring, she enjoys spending time at home with her husband in the garden.

www.ingramcontent.com/pod-product-compliance
Lightning Source LLC
Chambersburg PA
CBHW022156260626
47155CB00018B/2240